A CAFFEINE HIT

HAUNTING AVERY WINTERS

BOOK VI

DIONNE LISTER

Dionne Lister

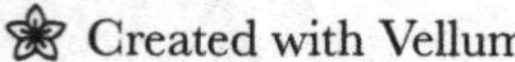 Created with Vellum

This book is dedicated to one of my gorgeous readers. Jackie C, I'm sorry I made you burn all those saucepans. I didn't mean to. Honest. Now, please go check the dinner before it happens again.

CHAPTER 1

Coffee. I can't live without it, which has just become a problem. This morning, I have to brave going into Heavenly Brew and seeing my nemesis, Joyless. Not my preferred way to start my day, especially after she stirred up trouble against me with that Facebook post, and her brother got a warning from the police for vandalising my car. Unfortunately, I'd run out of coffee grounds at home and didn't have time to get more from the supermarket, return home to make it, then get to my first interview.

So seeing Joyless it was.

Hopefully the substandard morning wasn't going to set the tone for the rest of the day. At least when I stepped past the middle-aged male ghost in a dark tailored suit who'd just walked out of Heavenly Brew and was staring inside, it smelled delicious. Brewing coffee was one of my favourite scents in the whole world. I couldn't really blame that ghost for watching the customers get their coffees. My eyes widened. How could I survive the afterlife if I couldn't taste and enjoy coffee? That was extra incentive for not dying anytime soon.

Okay, so there were more important ones, but that was on the top-ten list I kept in my head.

There were two customers who'd ordered and were awaiting beverages, and another man stood at the cash register, ready to order. My nemesis was the only person on this morning, and her scowl confirmed she wasn't happy. At least time went quickly when you were flat out. But typical Joyless to be lacking, well, joy.

The twenty-something guy waiting to order was dressed in a suit, his arms folded. I'd seen him in here a few times before. "You have to be the slowest server ever." Hmm, he didn't normally say much. Looked like he wasn't in a great mood today.

Joyless looked up from what she was doing. Her mouth dropped open. Then she squinted at him. "And that, ladies and gentlemen, is one of the reasons I broke up with this twat." A forceful breath whooshed out of her mouth. "I can't believe I ever dated you. Lucy can have you for all I care."

The guy placed his hands on the counter. I kind of felt sorry for him. How desperate did you have to be to date Joyless in the first place, let alone have her break up with you? He didn't realise what a favour she did him. Also, while her daggers were aimed at him, I was left injury free. What a relief. "*You* broke up with *me*?" His snide laugh bounced off the tiled floors and the stainless steel coffee machine. "That'll be the day. Also, when are you going to pay me back the money I lent you? I've been waiting three months. Last time I was in here, you said you would have the money for me today. So where is it?"

It was Joyless's turn to plant her hands on her hips. "I did no such thing. You gave me that money! Show me the piece of paper that says it was a loan?" He said nothing. "Right. Thought so." She finished with the coffees she was making, and the customers took them with a wary look at her before hurrying out, eager to escape the crossfire. "Right, so your usual—almond-milk decaf with a shot of caramel?"

"Yes. And you'll be hearing from my solicitor about that money. I gave you plenty of warning, but I'm done."

She rolled her eyes and bent to grab a cup from under the counter. She made his coffee, and he handed over the money. Joyless put it in the till and stared at him. "Go on, then. Taste it and make sure I haven't made a mess of it. Last time, you complained I'd boiled the milk. The time before that, the milk was too cold. Maybe I should call you Goldilocks?" Her hip cocked out as she stared at him, almost daring him to drink it and complain.

He gave her a look that said "challenge accepted." The first sip was tentative—and who could blame him. It would be like her to boil the milk so he burnt his mouth. He narrowed his eyes and took a bigger sip. His forehead furrowed. The cup fell from his hand, coffee splattering everywhere. His hand clutched his chest as he collapsed. By the time Joyless hurried from behind the counter, he was having a seizure.

She stared down at him. "Stop being stupid, Alan. You're going to scare the customers away." She looked up at me and rolled her eyes. "Argh, never mind."

I didn't bite because I was pretty sure it wasn't an act. His lips were blue, his skin ashen. He fitted while I called nine, nine, nine. When I got off the phone, he stilled, and his ghost appeared next to me, surprise on its face. Oh, brown bananas. Why was I always there when stuff happened? At least there was one other customer who'd walked in when he'd taken possession of his cup. Surely no one could blame me for this one?

Alan stared at his dead body and blinked. "What happened?" He was likely talking to himself because he hadn't looked at me. He moved his gaze to what he probably thought was his own real body and patted his chest and down to his thighs. He frowned. "How can I be in two places at once? This doesn't make sense."

Pushing my questions for Alan aside, I licked my bottom lip and focussed on Joyless. "He's dead."

Horror crossed her face. "What do you mean? How do you even know? You haven't felt for a pulse."

I shook my head. "I'm not touching anything. Can't you see his skin and lips are the wrong colour? His chest isn't moving either. Why don't *you* feel for a pulse?"

She shook her head and folded her arms. "I'm not doing it. I bet you killed him with a poison dart or something. You're trying to make me look guilty."

I sighed and gave her a withering look. "I'm pretty sure he's your ex. Why would I do you such a favour? Seems to me that you're the one who benefits when he dies. He won't be chasing you for money. I don't even know the guy."

Her eyebrows rose to heights I was sure they'd never before seen as realisation sunk in. Death was horrible, but I found it low-grade amusing that she hadn't considered that he might have just had a heart attack and died of natural causes. Although that seizure might mean he'd been poisoned. Or maybe.... "Was he an epileptic?" It would've been better if I could've asked him directly, but I wasn't about to give myself away in front of Joyless... although. Hmm.

"Not that I know of."

The approaching sirens got louder.

"I can't be dead. I'm healthy."

I side-eyed Alan, and he finally noticed me. I gave a small head shake.

The woman who'd also been waiting to order slowly backed out of the door, then hurried away. I memorised her description so I could tell Bellamy to interview her later—forties, frizzy blonde hair to her shoulders, slim build, and about five foot three, dressed in black workout tights and a pink Puma T-shirt. I was not going to let Joyless pin this one on me.

Now the woman was gone, I decided that Joyless already had such a low opinion of me, and what did I care if she thought I was crazy. I turned to Alan's ghost. "Did your drink taste funny?"

He cocked his head to the side. "Maybe a little more acidic than usual. Can almond milk go off?"

Joyless's face morphed into anger. "Who the hell are you talking to? Are you trying to upset me?"

I turned to her. "I can assure you that I'm making no effort whatsoever. It's just an unintended benefit of me existing." I gave her a sarcastic smile and placed my attention back on Alan. "I guess so. Has Joyl—" Oops. Although did it really matter if she knew what I called her? Argh, I'd better not. Antagonising her too much was like waving a red rag in front of a bull. "Has Joy ever threatened you?"

He gave her a dirty look. "When I broke up with her, she threatened to cut my bollocks off and feed them to her dog. There was also that time, when we got together, that she said she'd smash my phone if I kept in touch with an ex of mine. She has violent tendencies." He peered at me. "You don't think she killed me, do you?" At least he'd accepted that he'd died. But, dur, she seemed like the prime candidate. Was he usually this slow, or was it the shock of having just died that had short-circuited his powers of deduction?

I flipped my hands over so my palms faced the ceiling. "I have no idea. Has anyone else threatened you lately? Do you have any enemies?"

The ghost who'd been waiting outside walked in, the paramedics running in behind and through him with a bag of equipment. It was getting crowded in here. One of the paramedics knelt to take a pulse. He looked up at his female partner and shook his head. The female paramedic looked at me. "What happened?"

"He had some coffee, then clutched his chest, fell to the ground, and fitted."

The ghost laughed, fat stomach jiggling with mirth. His oily combover didn't add anything pleasant to the visual. "Just as planned." He rubbed his hands together. "The boss will be happy when I tell him." His raspy voice sounded just like an American mafia guy, except for the Cockney English accent.

I didn't say anything, but I looked at him.

Surprise lit in his expression before his mouth turned up in a smile as oily as his hair. "You can see me? Interesting. Keep your mouth shut, lady. All you need to know is that this bird did it." He jerked his chin towards Joyless and snickered. I narrowed my eyes. My gut told me he was lying. I doubted that Joyless was "the boss"; besides, she couldn't see ghosts, and this ghost being here and saying that made me think he was here to report back to his boss. I swallowed. There was someone else near here who could see ghosts? I squeezed my hands into fists. The need to ask this guy questions overwhelmed me. But the paramedics were here, chatting quietly.

I stared at the ghost. He inclined his head in a goodbye. I shivered at the gleam in his eyes. Then he disappeared. Argh!

The male paramedic turned to me—at this stage, Joyless was pale and had taken a seat behind the counter. Whether she was shocked at seeing a dead body or the fact that she'd dated him, I couldn't say. I had doubts that she could care about anyone enough to get upset at them dying. When she died, though, she was probably going to have an absolute meltdown. That thought was comforting in a way. I should be ashamed, but I wasn't. You reaped what you sowed, so they said. "This could be a suspicious death, so we can't move the body until the police give us the all-clear. Do you think you and the other lady could wait out of the way for them? I'm sure they'll have questions for you."

"Of course."

Speaking of the devil, Sergeant Bellamy strode through the door. He gave a nod to the paramedics; then his gaze fell on me. His brows rose. "Miss Winters, on the scene again, I see."

I gave him a "what can you do" look. "I'm nothing if not consistent." Which reminded me—I hadn't had my coffee, and I had an interview to get to. "Sergeant, I hate to seem heart-less, but I need to leave. I have an interview soon, but I'd be happy to come by the station on the way back and give my statement."

"Give me the quick version now, and then you can go." He looked down at the body, then back at me. "I'm going to be here a while. Come by the station at one."

"Okay, will do." I went over everything that had happened since I'd walked through the door, minus the ghost stuff.

When I was done, he said, "I see. He turned his head and spied Joyless behind the counter. "Miss Stick, do you mind having a chat?"

She stared at him silently but stood and came out from behind the counter. When I'd told him what happened, I'd forgotten about the type of milk he'd had. "Sergeant Bellamy?" He peered over from the table he sat at with Joyless. "The deceased had an almond-milk coffee. The container is still here and the jug with some left."

"Thank you, Miss Winters." He turned to one of the two officers who'd come in after him. His nod to PC Patel was firm. "The coffee machine, the cups, all the milk, everything is to be bagged and taken away as evidence."

"Yes, sir." Patel put on rubber gloves and stepped in behind the counter. "Miss Winters."

"Hello, PC Patel. How's everything this morning?"

He shrugged one shoulder. "The usual. You're in the thick of it again."

I smiled. "The universe seems to think it's funny to place me wherever dead bodies are going to turn up. I've come to terms with it now; although some people in the village think I'm a harbinger of death. What can you do?"

He chuckled. "Indeed. Well, have a nice day." He collected the tetra pack of almond milk and placed it in a plastic bag, sealed it, and set it on the counter.

"I'll try. You too." Oh well, no coffee for me this morning. I'd have to wait and have the horrible instant crap at the office.

I gave a reluctant look to Alan—I had questions that I couldn't ask right now—then stepped out into the overcast day.

As I walked to my car, I wondered how that gangster and his boss fit into all of this and sighed. Just another action-packed morning in my life. I could do with boring about now and a smooth-flavoured coffee, but I had a feeling what I wanted in this life didn't count because the powers that be weren't listening.

CHAPTER 2

Clothed in a black knee-length dress, black stockings, and pink slippers, a woman I assumed was Rosa Kanellopoulos answered the door with a scowl. The just-north-of-middle-aged woman did not look happy to see me. Argh, not again. When could we go back to the good old days of people being happy to see me when I showed up for a story? "What do you want? I don't want to buy Tupperware or change religions." She started to shut the door.

"I'm from the *Manesbury Daily*" was all I could get out before the door closed. I sighed. Now I'd have to find another story to cover.

The door opened. A bright smile had replaced the scowl. "Oh, sorry, darling. Are you Avery Winters?"

I smiled, my shoulders loosening in relief. "Yes, Ms Kanellopoulos. I'm here to do the article on your cat-breeder complaint."

"Please come in." She opened the door and started down the brown-tiled hallway. I pulled the door to after myself and followed. She led me through her neat-and-tidy home to a back patio.

Under an awning sat a dark brown, round, two-seater timber table with two black iron chairs. On the table sat a gorgeous ruddy-coloured Abyssinian kitten. It stood and looked at me. When I approached the table, it walked to the edge and head-butted my stomach. "What a gorgeous kitty." I stroked its head, down its neck, to its back.

Rosa folded her arms and looked put out. Her annoyed tone was confirmation of her mood. "That's Zeus. He's the reason I wanted you to write an article about Horizon Cattery."

I frowned. "Oh, is there something wrong with him, and they won't give you your money back?" When she called the paper, she said she wanted to make a complaint, otherwise I would've thought she wanted to recommend them—this cat was so pretty and affectionate. It seemed to have everything in the right place too—four legs, two ears, tail…. What could be wrong?

"I wanted a cat who would catch mice and sit on my lap every now and then. This kitten wants constant affection, and he's into everything. He wakes me up at three in the morning to play. I lock him in the laundry at night now, and he scratches the door incessantly and whines." She gripped her head with both hands. "I can't take it any more, and they won't take him back."

I didn't know a lot about breeders, but I did know that in Australia, at least, any good breeder would take back an animal that wasn't working out. "That doesn't sound very ethical. Surely they want the best for their animals?"

"It doesn't seem like it. So, I'd like to do an article on that, and can we see if we can rehome Zeus?"

The cat stood on his hind legs and put his front paws on

my chest. I stared down into his huge green eyes, then picked him up. He nudged under my chin, and a loud, rumbly purr vibrated out of him. "He's pretty adorable. I'd take him, but my landlady doesn't allow pets."

She stared at me. "He seems to like you, but then again, he likes everyone."

I chuckled. "Thanks for the compliment."

She smiled. "Sorry, but you know what I mean. And I feel bad for wanting to give him up, but I'm not cut out to be a needy-pet parent." If only she'd done more research before buying him. I was sure I'd read somewhere about Abyssinians being one of the more intelligent breeds. They also loved to explore, and many owners walked them on a lead. I didn't have any sympathy for Rosa, but I had plenty for the soft bundle purring in my arms.

I really was sorry I couldn't take him. "You're such a cutie, aren't you." I pulled one of the chairs out and sat far enough from the table so the kitten could curl up in my lap. I got my notepad and pen out of my bag. "So, let's get to it. Tell me what happened, and then I want to do a write-up on Zeus. We want to make sure we get the right person taking him on."

"Thank you so much, Avery. I appreciate it."

After twenty minutes, we were done with the questions and photos. Rosa waited till we were at the door to drop her bombshell question. When I tried to hand Zeus to her, she stepped back. "Could you take him, please?"

"What? No. I told you that I can't have any animals in my place." It was awkward holding the cat out, so I cuddled him to me again. The poor little guy. I placed a kiss on the top of his head, lest he understood what was going on and felt unwanted, which he kind of was. Why were people so horrible? How could she not have fallen in love with him?

"Please, Avery. I can't handle this any more, and I'm

leaving the country tomorrow to visit Greece. My mother's ill, and they need me there. I have no one who can look after him."

I blinked. Was she kidding me right now?! "What are you going to do with him if I don't take him?" I shouldn't even be asking, but there was no way I could just walk out and leave him to her mercy. I was such a sucker. Maybe Meg could mind him for a few days until the story was out and we found someone to take him?

She shrugged. "I was thinking of dropping him to the shelter, but he would have a better chance of finding a good home if he goes with you and there's an article about him. I really thought this was the best thing I could do for him. And if you can't find him a place, you can take him to the shelter." Argh, the best thing she could've done for him would be to keep him. Jeeze. Not to mention, she was dumping the whole problem onto me. So now I was meant to feel bad if I couldn't rehome him. It would be me waving goodbye as I hurriedly dumped him in the animal equivalent of foster care. Zeus picked that moment to lick my jaw. I sighed, and Rosa smiled. "Just wait here a moment, and I'll get his stuff. Thank you, Avery! You're the best."

I didn't know if I was the best, but I was pretty sure I was the biggest pushover. I peered down at the cat in my arms. "Well, Zeus, looks like it's me and you, kid." At least until I could find him somewhere to live, and it better be before the end of today because Mrs Crabby wasn't going to be suckered in by his cute little face. Maybe if he'd been some kind of hellhound, she'd have felt an affinity… if she were capable of feeling an affinity with anyone or anything. But I doubted that. Mrs Crabby was an island… in a ring of fire, on a planet with more deadly creatures than Australia.

Rosa returned with a garbage-bag's worth of paraphernalia, and we placed Zeus into his cat carrier. He didn't seem too worried—maybe he was as keen to leave as she was to get rid of him. As I pulled out of my parking spot and headed for the office, I couldn't help thinking I was crazy. Who just takes a cat with no notice and agrees to rehome him? "Zeus, what if I can't find someone to take you? How am I supposed to leave you at the shelter?"

A meow came from the back seat, as if he were saying, "Don't worry. I know you'll do your best."

"I will do my best, kitten. I promise. I just hope it's enough."

❧

I carried Zeus in his carrier, two bowls, and a packet of dry food into the MacPherson Media building. As I passed the reception area, Joyless's equally evil sister called out, "Is that an animal you have there, Winters?" She shot out of her seat and hurried to stand in front of me, hands on her hips, halting my progress.

"I'm not sure. You tell me."

She narrowed her eyes and stared into the carrier. "Yes. It's a cat." She looked at me. "You know damned well it's a cat. There are no animals allowed in the office. Get it out right now." Wow, she never ever acknowledged me, but as soon as she had an opportunity, she was here to smack me down.

"I'm sorry, but I'm taking him to the office. It's just for today. The woman I just interviewed foisted him onto me. I didn't have a choice."

"I don't care. If you don't leave this instant, I'm calling Julian."

I cocked my head to the side. "You know what? I'm not

sorry. You call Julian, and while you do that, I'm going up to the office with Zeus."

Her brows rose. She stepped into my space and put her arms out. "I'm not letting you past."

I laughed. Was she for real? Why was I surrounded by idiots? Okay, so not totally surrounded—it was more of a fifty-fifty ratio. "Do you really want me to walk into you?"

"You won't."

"Why wouldn't I?"

"Because I'll have you charged with assault." Her smug face was as encouraging as if she'd been gesturing and inviting me to keep going. So I did. I walked into her, but she wouldn't budge. I made more effort, and she moved backwards, until her heel hit the stairs, and she fell onto her backside. "Ouch!"

I stepped around her and went upstairs, ignoring her threats to call the police. When I reached the doorway, Carina was there gazing out. "Avery! What was all d'at racket?"

"My favourite receptionist was being an elephant's behind."

She peered at the things in my hands. "Oh my, what's d'at?"

"Let me come in, and all will be revealed. And can you shut the door?" I didn't want Zeus escaping when I let him out.

She stepped out of my way, by which time Finnegan was staring at us. I put everything on the ground behind my desk while Carina shut the door and came over. I opened the cat carrier, lifted Zeus out, and held him to my chest. He purred and nudged his head under my chin, which seemed to be a signature move of his. I grinned. Kitten cuddles were the best thing ever. "I present to you, Zeus, the cat who needs a new home."

Finnegan jumped out of his seat and rushed over, by which

time Carina was already grabbing at the kitten. "Oh, can I have a hold? He's adorable." I passed him over because he seemed happy to go. "Little cutie. You are so soft and squishy." She looked at me as Finnegan patted Zeus. "But how did you end up wit' him? He's an Abyssinian, isn't he? D'ey're expensive. I had a friend who bought one a couple of years ago, and she paid fifteen hundred pounds back d'en."

I gave them the rundown on what happened at Rosa's place. Finnegan grinned. "You're a soft touch, Lightning."

"I know, but I couldn't just walk out and leave him. Look at that face." My baby-talk voice was well and truly activated.

Finnegan laughed. "You're a gonner. Why don't you take him?"

"Two words—Mrs Crabby. She doesn't allow pets, and she hates me as it is. I mean, I could try, but you'd have to be willing to let me rent one of your bedrooms when it all goes to hell."

Carina laughed. "Ooh, you two should move in toged'er."

Finnegan's brow furrowed. "Why? That's so random, C."

She snuggled her face against Zeus's. "You make a good team." She winked. Okay, so I wouldn't be totally against moving in with him, but it would end badly because I was pretty sure that my superpowers that kept me from giving into how I felt and asking him out would crumble if I never had a break from him. And then he'd be disgusted and ask me to move out, and then I'd be homeless and have to move to another village. Okay, so that escalated quickly, but I needed the reality check. *Thanks, brain.*

Finnegan and I shared a look and shook our heads. He turned back to the cat. "Can I have a hold, please? You're hogging the cuteness." Carina mumbled something in cute speak and reluctantly passed him to Finnegan. The cat immediately purred and nuzzled him. So much for feeling special that Zeus had taken to me so easily, but then again, Rosa did say he was too affectionate. Was that even a thing for pets? I could get it in humans—I needed space sometimes. If someone was too clingy, that was going to put me off, but a pet? That's what you wanted—someone to cuddle and snuggle up to, like a living soft toy. Not only squishy and fluffy, but also warm, and in Zeus's case, purry.

The door flew open, and Julian burst through the doorway in his usual enthusiastic fashion. He was already on the lookout and seemingly spied what he was after. "Ah, there it is. I was told there was an animal in the building. Can I see?" Yikes. Was he going to insist I get Zeus out? Surely he'd be more reasonable than his unhinged receptionist.

Finnegan smiled and passed the cat to Julian. "His name is Zeus. Lightning has to find him a home."

Julian looked down at the ruddy bundle of fur. "Aren't you just the cutest. I'd love to take you, but my wife's allergic." He put on a baby voice. "Look at that face. Ooh, what a gorgeous face." He rubbed his chin on the top of Zeus's head, and the purring got louder. Carina and I shared a smirk.

The *click-clack* of high-heeled footsteps echoed outside the door, and the receptionist of doom stood in the opening. "See, I told you she brought a cat in here." Her triumphant smug expression fell when Julian lifted the cat and rubbed his face on his belly. I bit my lip and forced back a laugh. A small snort escaped. She turned a glare my way.

I smiled. "Ah, Julian, Ms Stick told me that I wasn't allowed to have animals in the building, but I had no choice but to bring him in. The lady at the last interview foisted him on me. She was going to take him to the shelter, but she thought I'd have a better chance at rehoming him, especially since I'm going to put that in the article."

He pulled his face out of the cat's belly and cuddled him.

Luckily, he was wearing one of his ridiculous Hawaiian shirts today, and the fur was invisible against the red-and-orange floral pattern. Julian turned to Bethany. She folded her arms and cocked her hip out. "Animals are a health hazard in the workplace. Avery needs to get rid of that mangy cat right now."

I raised a brow. There was nothing mangy about Zeus at all, but I didn't say anything because arguing with her in front of the boss would just make me look petty.

I needn't have worried because Julian was a decent person. "Bethany, this is the most adorable kitty ever. I have no problem with Avery bringing it in. Look at the smiles on everyone's faces. It's good for morale." Ooh, she didn't like that. Her face screwed up in distaste. Julian turned to me and handed Zeus back. "If you need to bring him in tomorrow as well, that's not a problem. But if he makes any messes, you're to clean them up properly. Understood?"

I grinned. "Yes, M… Julian. Definitely." It was still weird calling him by his first name.

"Out of interest, Winters, why can't you take him?"

"My landlady doesn't allow pets. It's going to be sad to give him to someone else, though. He's growing on me already." I stroked his back. It wasn't just the Mrs Crabby thing—it wouldn't be responsible for me to get a pet in England. When my life here was over—I ignored the fear that sliced through me at that thought—and I eventually had to return to Australia, trying to get him through quarantine was a big deal. I didn't know the exact time, but animals coming into Australia had to be quarantined for around three to six weeks. I couldn't do that to him or any animal. It would be awful for them. "I'm going to miss him." I looked at Zeus. "I'll make sure you go to someone super nice. You deserve to have a wonderful life." Call me crazy, but tears welled in my eyes. I blinked them away and cleared my throat.

"Okay, then. Show's over. Enjoy your day, kids. See you later." Julian turned and left. Abrupt as ever but kind.

Bethany's eyes narrowed, and I smiled at her. "Bad luck. Your desire to cause trouble has failed. Ta, ta." I waved Zeus's paw at her in goodbye, then my foot nudged the door shut in her face.

Carina burst out laughing. "Oh my God, Avery. D'at was wonderful."

"It was satisfying. Petty but satisfying." I sniggered. Okay, so I didn't like the person the Stick sisters turned me into sometimes, but lying down and taking their abuse without any pushback was a recipe for continued harassment. New, stronger Avery wasn't taking that crap any more.

Zeus wriggled to get down, so I obliged, placing him on the floor. He sniffed my ankles before moving to Finn's feet and to the door. We watched him explore his new surroundings. Eventually Finnegan looked at me. "So… now that excitement's over, what happened this morning? I heard that Joy might be charged with murder. I can't believe it. Other than that stuff she pulled with you the other week, she's not that bad. It's a big jump from harassment to murder." He didn't love Joyless, but he still didn't get how bad she really was. Him sticking up for her right now while probably logical because he'd known her for so long, felt like a betrayal. She'd given me so much grief, and if the situation had been reversed, I would've hated on her so much.

My workmates stared at me, waiting for the scoop, which reminded me—I could write about what happened for the paper. I wouldn't name names, though, just report on the event. The fact that I disliked Joyless would mean I'd have to be careful of what I said. Being charged with libel wasn't my idea of fun, not to mention that I was a journalist, and remaining impartial and reporting only facts was important. Also, the facts made her look pretty guilty, but there was a big but. Who was that ghost, and did he work for the real murderer? I'd have to speak to Charles later, see if we could track this ghost down.

I gave them the short version. "Which reminds me—I need a coffee ASAP, even if it is the instant crap in the kitchen." I shuddered.

Carina twirled her magenta hair around her finger. She bit her bottom lip. "I hate to mention it, but you didn't just find a dead body—you were d'ere when it happened… again. You really have bad luck, lovie. Are you okay?"

I didn't want to ignore the hint that it was weird, because it was, and I didn't want my friends wondering and questioning why I was always at those scenes. "I'm fine. It wasn't pleasant, but I didn't know him, and I'm kind of getting used to it." It made it easier knowing that these people didn't just die and end. I might also just push the shock of it out of the way to deal with later. Thinking about it over time helped me process. The worst one had been Simone, the hairdresser. Even though we'd gotten justice, I still had the occasional nightmare. At least I could talk about it with Charles and Naomi, the other woman who'd been murdered by the same people. For some reason, she hadn't transitioned to the next place. Her boyfriend, Kyle, was still pretty cut up about her death, and I'd agreed to pass Naomi's messages onto him every couple of weeks. I usually called him, and we chatted. It was weird, but it made them happy. As much as Naomi didn't want him to move on with someone else, she knew he would need to one day, and she was trying to help him get over her as quickly as possible. I didn't have the heart to tell her that talking to him all the time might just make him stay stuck in the past. But who was I to know whether that was the right or wrong thing? Maybe their love was meant to last, literally, forever? So, for now, I would facilitate their communication because I wanted them to be at peace. "And, yes, I'm well aware it's weird that I'm there when these things have just happened or, apparently now, are in the middle of happening. It wasn't my fault, and there are witnesses to prove it." I hoped my words didn't sound too annoyed because I wasn't. I was just… wary.

Carina gave me a hug. "It's okay. We don't t'ink d'at, but after what happened wit' Joyless last time, I know you'd be t'inking it. And it is… unusual."

I sighed. "It is. Maybe being hit by lightning gave me some kind of superpower or something?" My laugh was nervous. Maybe I could start hinting at who I really was. Sergeant Bellamy hadn't had a meltdown when I told him. Would some of my friends be understanding too?

Finn folded his arms. "Next you'll be saying you can talk to ghosts or something equally as dodgy. It's just coincidence. I'd say it's bad luck." Ooookay, so maybe my friends wouldn't be anywhere close to understanding. One friend in particular. The friend whose opinion mattered the most. I hated myself for my crush and for the way my stomach dove to the floor. There was no coming clean to Finn in this lifetime.

"Ha, yeah, bad luck. At least it's given me plenty of stories. Um, don't take that the wrong way. I wouldn't go that far to get a story, but if I have to think of it any way, I'd prefer it to be positive." Yikes. If I wasn't careful, they'd soon be on team Joyless and be accusing me of killing people.

Carina dropped her arms. "Don't worry, Avery. We know you're not killing people. It is strange, but maybe d'e universe puts you d'ere for a reason. You have managed to help solve every single murder. I t'ink whatever d'e reason, it's good.

You've helped so many people since you came here. I'm proud to call you a friend."

I smiled. "Thanks, C. Ditto." My gaze travelled from her to Finn. "And you, too, even if you're a bit of a curmudgeon sometimes." I gave him a cheesy grin. "Anyway, it's time for me to have my horrible coffee, which is better than no coffee." And after that, I was going to get back to work. I had a home to find for the cutest cat in Manesbury and reality to ignore.

When I finally started dating again, it would never be to Finn. Which was more depressing than it should be. It was time to get over it because a lifetime of regret wasn't one to look forward to. I'd overcome so much to get where I was, and I could do anything I set my mind to.

I really could.

No, really.

CHAPTER 3

At lunchtime, I'd gone to the Frog and Trumpet to see if Meg wanted to adopt the cutest pussycat ever. She'd apologised, but the answer had been no. She was worried about him getting into the dining area or kitchen. They didn't have time to watch over him and avoid a visit from the Food Standards Agency. She also didn't have the time for him she thought he deserved. I understood, but it didn't make it any easier. I'd left him at the office with Finn while I drove to see Sergeant Bellamy at the station.

Patel was at the front desk today. "Hello, Miss Winters. Can I help you?"

"I'm here to see Sergeant Bellamy about this morning. I have to give a proper statement." And give it in private. I hadn't had a chance to speak to Charles yet, but he would never say no to helping me. In fact, he might be here with Sergeant Fox. This was going to be weird, laying it all out there and facilitating conversations between Bellamy and the spirit world. Since I'd told him, he hadn't said anything or asked any questions. He might be waiting for me to talk about it in my own time. Or had his kindness and understanding been fake in as much as he was being nice but didn't truly believe me? Did he think I was bonkers? Possibly. Patel buzzed me through, and second thoughts hammered my confidence until it was dripping off me in large pieces, nothing more than a fish-scale-sized fragment remaining by the time I reached Bellamy's office door.

I knocked, my heart pattering double time.

"Come in." When I entered, Bellamy gave me a small smile. "Ah, Miss Winters, thanks for coming by." I was about to shut the door. "Can you please leave it open just a crack? The heating's not working properly, and my office is chilly."

"Of course. I didn't realise English people ever got cold. It's not like it's snowing outside." I left the door open a smidge and sat. He was right, though. Despite my fitted slacks, the seat was cool on my bottom and thighs.

He chuckled. "It's not often I feel the cold, but that flu I had last week knocked me for six." Sergeant Fox and Charles appeared next to Bellamy's chair. They both said hi. I bit my bottom lip and looked between them and Bellamy. "Are you all right, Miss Winters?" Bellamy's concerned eyes gave me a tiny amount of confidence and reminded me of his understanding words three weeks ago when I'd revealed my secret.

"A couple of"—I lowered my voice—"ghosts just said hello."

His eyebrows rose. My palms sweated. Was his sympathy limited to when my life was in danger? "Who, and where are they?" He tentatively looked behind his chair.

I allowed a small breath to escape my lips. Was it possible that he'd still be kind in the face of my weirdness? Charles's eyes bugged out. "Wow, you're really coming clean about everything."

I nodded. "Just next to your chair." I pointed. "Sergeant

Fox, who worked here a very long time ago, and Charles, a young boy who died way before I was born. They're both very nice, and they've helped me a lot." I wasn't going to elaborate on the fact that they told me things that Bellamy wouldn't. He might be more secretive, thinking they're watching, and then I'd never find anything out that he didn't want me to know.

He turned his head and stared at what appeared to be an empty space next to his chair. He frowned and waved his hand through Sergeant Fox's stomach. Fox's lips turned up in a wry smile. Bellamy narrowed his eyes and did it again, then turned and waved his hand over his desk. "Hmm, it feels colder in that spot. I'm afraid that I can't say for sure whether what you're saying is true."

A sigh escaped. "I know I look like a nutcase. It's frustrating."

Charles looked at Fox. "Why don't you tell Avery what happened this morning when the door was closed? He'll have to believe her then."

Fox regarded him for a moment. I wasn't sure what the hesitation was about.

"Sergeant Fox, please don't tell me anything I don't want to know."

Bellamy stared at me, mouth slightly open. He wanted to believe me, but he wasn't quite there yet… or at least he wasn't quite ready for me to chat to ghosts in front of him. I'd have to give him the benefit of the doubt and hope that he would soon be a hundred per cent on board with the talking-to-ghosts thing. "Is he answering?" Bellamy asked.

I smiled. "Not yet. He's considering."

Fox looked at the ceiling, then back at me. "Okay, but he'll gather after this that we can feed you information."

"It can't be helped." That was something I'd been worried about, but there was no going back now.

"When Sergeant Bellamy got in this morning, he caught his finger between his chair arm and the table, and he swore a blue streak." Fox repeated the sentence word for word. "His door was closed at the time, so no one could've heard."

I pressed my lips together and did my best not to laugh. When I'd schooled my features, I looked at Bellamy. "Ah… Sergeant Fox says that you caught your finger between the chair arm and table this morning, and it hurt… a lot. So much so that you said…" I repeated what Bellamy had apparently said.

His eyebrows rose. Bellamy's mouth opened to say something, but nothing came out for a beat too long. Eventually, he said, "That's frighteningly accurate." He covered his mouth with his hand, thinking. "You might have bugged my office, but there's no way to hide a camera." His gaze raked each corner of the ceiling. He pushed his chair out and bent forward to peer under his desk before straightening and looking at me. "Okay." He stood. "Let's confirm this once and for all. I'm going to go into the men's bathroom and whisper something." He glanced at the space in which Fox and Charles stood. "This Sergeant Fox fellow can listen to what I say and tell you when we return."

I smiled. "Sounds good to me." I looked at Fox. "Is that okay?"

"Yes."

My gaze moved to Bellamy. "He said he's good to go."

"Right. I'll see you in a minute." Bellamy walked out, and Fox disappeared.

While they were gone, I looked at Charles. "I have a favour to ask."

He came and sat next to me. "Ask away."

I recounted the morning death and the ghost. "I was wondering if you could ask around, see who that gangster type is and who he's working for. As much as I don't like Joyless, this casts doubt on whether she did it. She might deserve punishment for other things, but if she's not guilty of murder, I'd hate to see her put in prison."

"Are you sure she's not guilty? It looks bad."

"It does. And Alan told me after he died that she'd threatened to cut his bollocks off and feed them to her dog. Shortly after they got together, she'd told him she'd smash his phone if he contacted his ex. She's definitely aggressive, and we know she loves to cause trouble, but that other ghost has given me loads of questions. I don't know if Alan's passed since this morning, but maybe you could try and find him, or at least find out if he's *gone* gone. We were interrupted before I could find out whether he had other enemies."

"Bellamy should be able to find that out from Alan's associates or family." Charles was right. It was probably more important that we found the thug guy.

Footsteps came from outside the slightly open door. "Miss Stick. Thank you for coming down. If you could wait a few moments, I'll be with you."

I jerked around to look out the door. Joyless stood there staring at me. Her eyes narrowed as if she was plotting something. Had she heard me "talking to myself" again? Not that it mattered. I'd done it in front of her this morning. There was nothing she could do to hurt me. Telling people I was crazy wouldn't make a dint in my friends' opinions of me… not like my family, who wanted to believe the worst of me.

Bellamy came in and shut the door. He sat and eyed me for a long moment before he said, "Okay, what did I say in the bathroom?"

Fox appeared next to Bellamy's chair. "He said 'the quick brown fox jumped over the lazy policeman and landed in a puddle.'"

I giggled. "Okay. I'm pretty sure that saying doesn't quite go like that." I looked at Bellamy and repeated Fox's words.

Bellamy swallowed and nodded slowly. "Right. You're right." He rubbed his chest. "You're right."

"I know it's a lot to take in."

He nodded. "Yes. I mean… I believed you when you told me a few weeks ago, but to be confronted with the reality." He took a deep breath. "I still haven't taken your statement, either, and I have to interview Miss Stick again. We're waiting on evidence from the lab, but it's not looking good for her."

"I bet it's not." I didn't know what else to say. I wasn't about to defend her until I knew for sure because maybe she did kill her ex, and the other ghost was trying to throw me off. I needed more information before I decided for sure one way or the other. The police might have found concrete evidence that showed she was innocent anyway, and then my input would be obsolete, except for trying to find the culprit. There was no love lost between me and Joyless, so I wasn't about to defend her without proof. It didn't make me petty—it made me cautious and reasonable. At least that's what I told myself.

"Can you give your statement to PC Adams, and if I need anything else, I'll let you know?"

"Yes, sure. And if you have any questions about the ghosts, let me know." That was kind of anticlimactic. I was expecting him to be more curious or worried or something. I'd been so nervous, yet nothing major had occurred as a result of me proving I could speak to ghosts. I stood.

He lifted his chin and peered up at me. "I'll be sure to. I was hoping to ask more questions right now, about Sergeant Fox, but real-world work must come first."

I smiled. "I understand. I'll speak to you later, then. Bye, Sergeant." I let myself out. As I walked past Joyless to PC Adams's desk, Joyless stared at me. Her face was void of expression, but I'd bet she was calculating ways of using my recent behaviour against me.

"Come in, Miss Stick."

She turned at Bellamy's request and went into his office, shutting the door behind her. Maybe it would be nice if my nemesis went to jail. It would be like a holiday for me. Imagine being able to go into the café every morning without the fear of being skewered by her sharp tongue or her death-ray glare.

As I gave my statement to PC Adams, the idea of having a life devoid of Joyless became more and more alluring. Was it wrong of me to hope she'd killed her ex and that she'd go to jail for a long time? Probably, so let's pretend I did nothing of the sort.

CHAPTER 4

Despite Julian fast-tracking my article on Zeus, no one had contacted me to adopt him by five that afternoon. I'd also called the breeder, but they declined to comment and refused to rehome him. They totally deserved the bad rap they were getting. Fair enough that Rosa was ridiculous for not wanting an affectionate cat, but Zeus had been more than she could handle activity-wise, and the breeder should want the best for their charges.

Carina and Finnegan were back in the office, and thank goodness for that because when it was time to go home, I didn't know how I was going to sneak Zeus in without Mrs Crabby noticing. She had a sixth sense where I was concerned. Always popping out of her front door to reprimand me for whatever she could think of when I was coming or going. She was scarier than a jack-in-the-box, which was saying something because they were creepy as hell.

Zeus was on my lap as I worked. He really was the most adorable kitty ever. If only there was accommodation I could afford that accepted pets. I checked the work email one last time. Zip. Bummer.

I gazed across the room at my friends. "Um, I have a favour to ask… to beg, really."

They both looked up, and Carina said, "What's up, lovie?"

I covered Zeus's ears. Chances were slim to none that he could understand me, but I didn't want to upset him, just in case. "I can't take him home with me. Mrs Crabby will pitch a fit and might use it as an excuse to kick me out. Can one of you take him just for tonight? You can bring him back here in the morning. No one's contacted us yet to adopt him, and Meg can't watch him. He has everything he needs—bed, food, bowls, penguin toy." I lifted him up and rubbed my cheek against his. "Look at this cute face."

Carina gave me a sad smile. "I'd love to, but my ferret wouldn't appreciate it. I'm so sorry."

I stared at her. "How did I not know you had a ferret?"

She shrugged. "It's not somet'ing I bring up randomly." She laughed. "I've had him for a year, but he's super territorial, and his teet' are sharp. It wouldn't end well." I cringed. One down. One to go. I settled Zeus on my lap and crossed my fingers and toes.

Carina and I stared at Finnegan. He looked at Carina, then me. "Why is everyone staring at me?"

"Read d'e room, Finny. You're d'e only one left. Anyway, it's only for one night. It's like a one-night stand. You're good at d'ose." Ooh, she was cheeky. I snorted at his offended expression.

He peered up at the ceiling and released a loud sigh that spoke of great burdens and the suffering of a thousand years. "Fine. I'll take him." He stood and came over.

I smiled. "Thank you. I owe you one. You really are the best."

"You don't have to flatter me now. I've already said yes."

"Okay, I take it back. You suck."

His mouth turned up on one corner. Argh, why did lopsided smiles increase a man's attractiveness tenfold? Or maybe it was just this man. My hormones were so dumb. They needed a talking to ASAP. "That's better." He collected Zeus from my lap, and other than giving me a surprised look, the cat seemed fine with the change of cuddler. "If you can get his stuff together and leave it next to the door, that would be awesome."

"Can do."

He put Zeus on his chair while he packed his laptop and notebook into his bag. I put Zeus's paraphernalia next to the door and took his carry case to Finn. I looked at Zeus. "I'm so sorry, cutie pie. I really wish I could take you home." I bent and kissed him on the top of his head and got a purr and head nudge for my trouble. My chest warmed. This cat was easy to fall in love with. Surely someone would contact us tomorrow about adopting him.

Finn opened the carrier door. "Okay, buddy. Sorry, but it's time to get in. Don't worry, though; it's a really short drive home." Being the perfect cat he was, he meowed once and elegantly stepped into the black-fabric carry bag. Finn zipped it up. "Good boy." Finn looked at me. "He's well trained for a kitten, or a cat even. They're not usually this well-behaved, are they?"

"I don't know. Probably not. I don't think Rosa trained him much, considering she didn't really like him or have time for him. Maybe he's just a smart cookie." I frowned. "I still can't believe Rosa didn't want you. Maybe you're just too smart for her. She needs a cat who doesn't think too much."

Finn grinned. "Ah, so you acknowledge that I'm suitable because I'm smart."

"Don't get too cocky, Vinegar. You're only suitable for one night, apparently. Unless you want to adopt him?" I couldn't keep the hope out of my eyes. It sounded crazy coming out of my mouth, but he didn't have a pet. Maybe he could adopt Zeus?

"Sorry, but I'm a one-night-only type of guy. Having a pet is a lot of responsibility."

"Cats aren't that bad. If you took him, I could feed him when you went away. And it's a safe area. You can probably let him roam during the day. He's practically no trouble. You probably wouldn't notice he was there until you were watching TV and he was sitting on your lap, all soft and purring." Okay, I was desperate to find the cat a good home where I could still visit him. So sue me.

He stared at me, a bemused expression in place. "Are you finished?"

"That depends. Will you adopt him, make him your firstborn?"

Carina peered at us, a smile ghosting her face. She was enjoying this immensely.

"I'm not ready for that kind of commitment, Lightning. I'm sorry." And he did look sorry as he cocked his head to the side, sadness clear in his eyes.

My shoulders slumped with my exhale. I looked at Zeus. "Well, I tried, cutie pie. Maybe I'll try Vinegar again tomorrow. You deserve the best home ever."

Finn put a hand on his heart, but there was genuine affection in his gaze. "I'm honoured that you think I'd provide the best home ever."

I shrugged, trying to come off as blasé. "You can afford to feed him, your home is clean, and you don't smell. What's not to like?"

Carina choked on her laughter. "D'at's not setting the bar too high."

I put my finger in front of my mouth and made a shushing gesture. "We don't want him to know."

"You ladies are killing me. Zeus and I are going home now. Do you want a lift, Avery?"

"Yeah, okay. Thanks." I'd been thinking about seeing if that obese ghost with the combover was loitering in front of the café, but chances were slim, and Charles was working on finding him anyway, so I might as well take the easy way home. And with Zeus taken care of for at least tonight, I could relax… sort of. It was hard not to worry about what tomorrow would bring on that front, though. Maybe Zeus's perfect owner would email me tomorrow morning, and we'd have him set up by the afternoon. Holding onto that thought, I packed my bag. "Bye, C."

"Bye, Aves. Have a good night. And don't worry. I'm sure you'll get lots of responses for Zeus tomorrow."

My smile was forced. "Yep. He's adorable. Who wouldn't want him, right?"

CHAPTER 5

The next morning, I rose at seven and went for a walk on the path that started at the end of our cul-de-sac and threaded through adjoining fields and abutted a forest. I didn't have my first interview until nine, and it was with the organisers of the Manesbury Fair, which was on towards the end of every November. There were two weeks to go, and they wanted to start drumming up interest to outsiders—it wasn't as if people in the village needed reminding. It was the event of the year, apparently. Local produce, homemade cakes, preserves, and cooking demonstrations, not to mention barnyard animals to pet, pony rides, and face painting, there was something for everyone.

About twenty-five minutes into my power walk, rustling came from the forest on my right. I stopped and turned, peering through the trees. It took my eyes a minute to adjust to the lower light under the early morning canopy. I sucked in a happily surprised breath. Two foxes were bouncing around, playing. I hurriedly lifted my phone and put it on video, hoping it would capture them in the dimness. How adorable!

One pounced on the other, and they rolled on the ground, wrestling. Their squeaky chatter and intermittent growling made me smile. I hadn't heard foxes before, and I'd only seen them trotting past on occasion from my window or when walking along the roadside. I'd also seen a squashed one on the road once, but I'd rather not think about that.

As the morning sun speared sideways between the trunks, something glinted near the playing fluffballs. Ooh, what was it? It could be rubbish, or it could be jewellery. What if it was an old Roman coin? It could be worth a fortune. It probably wasn't because I'd never be so lucky, but you never knew.

I didn't want to frighten the foxes, and I had no idea if they'd attack, so I said, "Hey, off you go." They jerked apart, both standing to face me, ready for action. "Shoo!" I waved my arms, and they turned and trotted off. Well, that was easier than expected. Foxes weren't vicious that I knew of, and many were probably used to people. If I'd had someone else with me, I might have tried to pat the foxes, but who knew, it might be the dumbest thing ever in the forest.

I walked in between the trees and a few scattered bushes. It wasn't foil or a discarded bottle top shining in the faint morning sun. I bent and picked up a silver heart locket on a broken chain. Soil had smudged in between the creases of the filigree, so it was hard to tell the pattern. I turned the locket over and rubbed dirt off the smooth back, revealing initials in flowing script. *EC.*

How long had it been here, forgotten, lost? Judging by the filthy coating, likely a few years at least. I was keen to get home and wash it. Before I headed back, I jammed my thumbnail in between the halves and forced them open. Whatever picture had been in there was browned; the image unrecognisable except for a bit of auburn hair on one side. It was almost

impossible to tell if was one or two people, or even only people. Maybe it was a person and their pet?

My walk back home was filled with thoughts about who might have dropped the locket. Would I be able to find them by putting something in the paper? It could be someone's most treasured possession, given to them by a cherished loved-one who was no longer around.

As I reached my front gate, Finn was coming out of his, Zeus on a leash, his tail straight up. Both of them looked at me. "Morning, Lightning."

"You're taking the cat for a walk?" I knew the harness was there for a reason, but I'd never seen someone walking a cat in real life. On Instagram it was par for the course, but it was always weirder to see something like that in person.

"What does it look like? Yes, I'm taking the cat for a walk."

"Why?" Seemed like a lot of work for someone who didn't want a cat. I would've thought he'd do the bare minimum. Was he even nicer than I'd given him credit for? That would make him super-duper nice since I already had a good opinion of him.

"He wouldn't shut up. Since five this morning. I tried patting him, feeding him, putting on the TV. He then found the harness and brought it to me."

My eyes widened. "Oh, wow. He's smart. No wonder Rosa thought he was hard work."

Zeus sniffed the ground, meowed, and pulled at the lead, trying to walk off. "You said it. I gotta go. See you at work later, when I can give you the cat back." Before I could answer, Zeus dragged him off, a bird in his sights. I took a quick video to show Carina later before chuckling and making my way quietly inside. There was no way I wanted to wake Mrs Crabby since it was still early. No noise before eight during the week and nine on weekends.

As I gently clicked the front door closed, a floorboard squeaked. Nooooo! I scrunched my eyes shut and froze.

Mrs Crabby's door flew open. Damn it! It was like she was waiting to catch me out. Okay, she was waiting—there was no doubt about it. "It's seven fifty. Why are you making such a racket?" She was still in her pyjamas and dressing gown. The dressing gown was pink and had a cute white goose on one lapel. It made her look less threatening, but I knew the truth. She was as vicious as an angry goose. The one on her clothes should've had its beak open and its tomia—the sharp cartilage on its tongue and beak—showing. Hmm, maybe geese were her spirit animal?

I swallowed my sarcastic words and resisted honking. Although, she might react to the call of the wild in a favourable way. "I'm sorry, Mrs Collins. I was trying to be quiet. I just went for a walk."

"Well, you tried and failed. How many times do I have to lay down the rules?" Her lips pinched together. "One of these days, you're going to push me too far, and I'll have to evict you." She shook her head slowly as if she was dealing with the biggest disappointment of her life. "I never should've rented out upstairs. What in the world was I thinking?" She stepped inside her apartment and forcefully shut the door. It wasn't a slam, exactly, but loud enough to show her displeasure. Whatever. I had better things to think about than the fact she was upset with me. She was always upset with me. Things were *normal.*

I jogged upstairs, not worrying about being quiet—that ship had sailed this morning. If I was going to get in trouble for things, I might as well do them.

As soon as I got inside, I went straight to the kitchen and washed and dried the locket. The filigree was gorgeous. Someone must be missing it. It seemed familiar somehow. Was it a common pattern? Come to think of it, one of my friends from school had one when I was a teenager, and I was sure it was similar. That must be why it felt like I'd seen it before. At least my memory was still good after being shocked to death by that stupid bolt, although there were some things from my old life that I'd love to forget.

I placed the locket on my dining table and took a picture of it. I'd put it in the paper with the proviso that if someone could tell me what was engraved on the back, I'd consider it theirs. I also had a quick look on Facebook and the wider internet to see if anyone had reported a locket missing in the last few years. Nope. Oh well, me posting it in the paper might get a result.

I also checked my work emails since I still had plenty of time to shower and dress and get to my first appointment. Ooh, three responses to my call-out for Zeus's adoption. The first one was a no. They wanted a barn cat to deal with mice. The cat wouldn't be allowed inside and would have minimal human interaction. That would not suit my cutie at all. He needed love and care.

The second and third emails seemed promising. One was a woman who had a small dog and lived in a ground-floor two-bedroom flat. She wanted another pet, so that seemed okay. The third was a man who said he wanted a kitten for his three children. The kids—aged three, six, and eight—had apparently been begging for a pet. Zeus struck me as a cat who would love the attention, and kids had more energy than adults. He was sure to get lots of pats and walks. This morning was looking up.

I showered, dressed, and packed my work bag, slipping the necklace into a safe, internal zippered pouch. The sun was out today, and even though the weather was cool, it was a lovely morning to walk. The town hall where I was meeting with the

Manesbury Fair committee was actually just at the end of the lane our office was on. After that, I was going to call the adoption candidates and make an appointment with the two suitable ones to come into the office to meet Zeus. I also wanted to meet the people and make sure they were safe to send my adorable boy home with. Okay, so he wasn't mine, but I felt responsible for him. In a different time and place, he could've been mine, a creature who would love me without judgement. Someone I could chat to who I could actually touch and was warm and cuddly. Not that my ghost friends weren't good company, but they lacked substance. Other than a quick hello or goodbye hug with my non-ghost friends, I couldn't remember the last time I cuddled up to anyone and watched a movie. Yes, Zeus was still just a cat, but he was real, squishy, and lovable. I sighed and slipped my bag over my shoulder. Wallowing never did anyone any good.

I made sure to stomp down the stairs. Sneaking didn't help, and since Mrs Crabby loved to get angry at me, I was giving her a gift really. When I reached the bottom of the stairs, her door stayed closed. I eyed it suspiciously, then opened the front door. Hmph, nothing. Maybe I should call her bluff more often. I shut the door noisily just for fun and headed off to work.

Heavenly Brew was still closed and marked off with police tape. Poor Anna. This was obviously bad for business. Had any of her equipment been affected? Would she have to get a new coffee machine? Was something like that even covered by insurance? I could imagine that phone call. "I have to make a claim because my one of my staff murdered someone, and the police confiscated my coffee machine." Yeah, nah. I didn't like her chances. Maybe I should check on her later. I didn't have her number, but maybe Meg or Carina did.

Alison De Luca, her frizzy blonde hair up in an explosive

ponytail was about to unlock her florist shop across the road. She noticed me and waved. "Hey, Avery! How are you?"

"I'm good, thanks." Ooh, maybe she wanted a cat. "Are you in the market for a pet?" I called across the street.

"What kind of pet?" She hadn't said no yet, so maybe it was a good sign?

"A cat. An Abyssinian to be exact."

Her face morphed into an apologetic expression. "I'm so sorry, but my wife's allergic, otherwise, I would say yes. I had cats growing up."

"Oh well, no worries. Have a good day." I waved, and she returned it. I tried not to stress—I still had two people to interview later, and chances were good that more applications would pop up in my email today.

I reached the laneway to the office, then strode past the MacPherson Media building. About a hundred and seventy feet away, at the end of the laneway, I reached the town hall. It was disappointing aesthetically, considering how quaint the village was. It looked to have been built in the 1950s and was a boring yellowish-brick, single-storey building. It had a couple of redeeming features—even though it was single storey, it was double height, and two Doric columns soared all the way to the higher-than-normal portico ceiling.

I strode through the tall, wide, green door into a terrazzo-floored foyer. The beige walls were about what I expected, and a noticeboard hung on the wall opposite the door. It had various pieces of paper attached, offering things from piano lessons and cooking classes to help with setting up your computer to plumber adverts.

An open door beckoned to my right. I peeked through to a vast, high-ceilinged room with a stage. This must be where they held town meetings and local drama performances. It probably got hired out for birthday parties and weddings too. Unfortunately, the group I was meeting wasn't in here.

I backed into the foyer. A corridor led off to my left, and a tall, lanky woman walked along it towards me. Her '60s-style blondish-grey beehive hairdo made her roughly-six-foot frame even taller. Even though she looked to be in her forties, I wouldn't be surprised if she was a long-distance runner. I could just imagine her in running shorts and a numbered singlet top. She smiled, wrinkles crowding at the corners of her eyes. "You must be Avery."

"I am. Lovely to meet you…?"

She held out a slim, long-fingered hand. "I'm Jenna Mathews. I head up the Manesbury Community Service Group. We organise fundraising for local community initiatives and run the Christmas, Easter, and spring events. It's lovely to meet you, Avery. You've been doing a wonderful job at the local newspaper. To be honest, since you're not from around here, I wasn't sure you'd capture the heart of the place in your interviews, but I was pleasantly surprised, not to mention what a help you've been to local law enforcement. We don't have our own police station, as you know, and, well, I think we don't get the best attention from the Cramptonbury mob."

That was the first I'd heard of anyone being unhappy with Sergeant Bellamy and his officers. I smiled politely—it wouldn't do to get her offside straight away, and she seemed to be nice; plus, she was giving me a compliment, which, given my history in this place, was roughly a fifty-fifty proposition. "Thank you, Ms Mathews."

She swiped a hand through the air. "Please call me Jenna."

"Ah, okay, Jenna. Why don't we get the interview started. I'd love to hear what you have planned for the fair." It was unusual that they were having a fair so close to Christmas, which they also had to organise. Talk about heaping it on yourself.

"Excellent. Come this way, Avery." She turned and headed back down the hallway.

We ended up in a room with an eight-seater timber table, whiteboard, sink, and sideboard. Coffee and biscuits were set up on the sideboard, and five people sat around the table—two men and three women. Everyone was over forty. One of the men and one of the women looked to be in their seventies. This was probably a great way for them to keep busy and connected.

Jenna introduced me, and everyone said hello, some more enthusiastically than others. The old man, Bob, and one of the middle-aged women, Trina she said her name was, were the less-enthusiastic ones. Were they relatives of Joyless maybe?

Jenna sat next to a middled-aged woman called Pat and gestured for me to sit next to her. At least Jenna seemed friendly. The man on my other side, Jonathan, seemed nice enough. He looked to be one of the youngest. His short brown hair and barely wrinkled face put him in his early forties.

Jenna had a small gavel. She bonked it lightly on a square of timber on a tea towel on the table. Rustically formal. I held in my giggle. At least I didn't feel out of my depth. "I'm calling this meeting to order. This is our third last meeting before the fair. I have my list." She held up a long, thin notebook. How long was this list? "We'll get to these outstanding items when Avery leaves. But until then, we'll give her our full attention and answer any questions she has about the fair."

The two I'd pegged as grumps gave me wary looks. The others nodded. I looked at Jenna. "Thanks so much." I turned to everyone else. "Thank you for welcoming me today. I'd like to start by finding out what the highlights of last year's fair were. Mentioning them in the article would be good to get people reminiscing and excited for what may happen this year." Pat started by telling me three things. Jenna told me another two, and then all was silent. "Great. So, what are the highlights of this year's festival?"

Hmm, who knew such an innocent question could be so divisive?

Pat smiled. "We're having a dog show this year for the first time."

Trina's lips squeezed together in a line. "I don't know why we couldn't have a cat show instead."

Jenna gave her a kind smile. "I know you wanted to enter Mr Mulberry, but we don't have the facilities for cats. We can hold the dog show outside."

Trina folded her arms and scowled. "Excuses, excuses."

It was time to step in. I didn't have all day to sit and wait. "What does the winner get, or is it just the kudos?"

Jenna's smile widened. "Oh, we have a great prize. A free grooming session with Ava Peron—she lives two villages over, but she has a successful business in Exeter. There's a two-month wait to get your dog in to see her."

"That's a great first prize." I wrote it in my notebook. "And what else do you think will be popular at the fair?"

Bob smoothed his eyebrows with one hand. "The produce display from our local farmers is always colourful and impressive. The winners for each category don't get a prize, but they gain free entry into the Devon Produce Show. Winners there receive money prizes, so it's popular."

"Okay, great." For a grump, at least he was answering my question.

Trina tipped her chin up and glared at me. "The cake-baking competition will be good. Our theme this year is vegetables."

Pat gave her a withering look. "So disappointing. We

should've had chocolate, like I'd suggested. Everyone loves chocolate."

Trina's tone was drier than the Simpson Desert. "I don't."

"Well, I'm allergic to zucchini, and I don't like pumpkin, so what cake can I even taste?" Pat was allergic to zucchini? Was that even a thing? I was going to google that later because it sounded impossible.

"Allergic to zucchini, so you say. You're just being ridiculous. If you don't like the taste of it, just be honest." Okay, so Trina was calling her out. I hoped she'd researched it because maybe it existed.

Jenna banged her gavel on the wood. "Now, now, ladies, let's just answer Avery's questions. We don't want her writing about our questionable behaviour, do we? The town might worry that we're bickering more than organising." Both women looked contrite. Jenna turned back to me. "Please don't put any of that in the article."

"Of course not. I'm actually looking forward to attending my first Manesbury Fair, and I bet everyone's excited to go." I didn't add that not much happened around here in terms of entertainment. It was probably one of the things residents counted down the days for. "So, what else have you got in store for the good residents of Manesbury?"

"It's all a bit of fun," Jonathan said, "so don't get the wrong idea, but we're having a fortune teller."

"More nonsense." Trina rolled her eyes. She was as much fun as a bag of rocks.

"That sounds like fun." And also a place I wouldn't go near. I had enough paranormal hijinks in my life. Besides, as much as I was no longer a sceptic about ghosts, people reading fortunes struck me as a scammy way to earn money. I'd been to one at a party once, and they'd been wrong about everything. It reminded me of horoscopes. They were always wrong when I looked them up. I guessed if they gave comfort and hope to people, maybe they weren't all bad, but I wasn't wasting my money on it.

Over the next twenty minutes, they told me about a few other things, and then that was it. "I've got plenty for my article now. Thank you. Can I take a photo of you all sitting here for the article?"

Everyone answered yes, except for Trina. It was Pat's turn to roll her eyes. "Fine, don't be in it, then. You can stand behind Avery while she takes the photo."

Trina's mouth fell open. "Oh, so you want all the credit."

"She didn't say that." Jenna's voice was gentle. "If you'd like to be in the photo, stay there. If not, you can stand with Avery, out of shot." I bit my lip to stop my smile. Crafty woman. That's probably why she led the group. If you gave someone a choice, they would find it very hard to argue. She just had to decide what she wanted.

Trina huffed. "Fine. I'll stay. But I'm going on record to say that I didn't want a photo."

"Your displeasure is noted," said Jenna.

I held my phone up. "Okay, everyone. Smile!"

❧

On my way back to the office, my phone rang—"Eye of the Tiger" played loudly. I'd added special ringtones for everyone, so I knew who it was. "Sergeant Bellamy, what can I do for you?"

"Miss Winters, I was wondering if you could spare thirty minutes to come to the station. I have a special request."

Huh? "A special request?"

"Yes."

"And you can't tell me now?" This was weird. He was usually pretty upfront.

"No. I'd rather talk to you about this face to face. So, can you come in?"

I didn't like the sound of this. Not that Bellamy would do anything bad to me, but my gut told me I'd be in for something I potentially didn't want. It made sense because why wouldn't he tell me? "If I agree to come in, I would like you to agree to let me in on the next big case you get." Despite moonlighting as the resident body finder, I was still a journalist, and I needed to earn money. Bellamy and I appeared to have found a truce since I told him about the ghosts, but he was good at making life difficult for me when I wanted information on crimes.

"Yes, definitely." Wow, that was too easy. Argh, seemed that I'd played right into his hands. What would I be walking into? "Okay, fine. I'll get my car and come down now."

"Thank you, Miss Winters. See you soon. Bye."

My first appointment with a potential Zeus adopter wasn't for another hour and a half, but since I wasn't going in straight away as I'd believed, I called Finn. "Hey, Vinegar, how's Zeus?"

"Hey, Lightning. He's good. We're in the office. Are you going to be here soon because I have to go to a story."

"That's kind of why I'm calling. Sergeant Bellamy's called me in urgently, so I won't be back for another forty-five minutes or so. I have the first potential family for Zeus coming in an hour and a half, so I have to be back for that."

"Right, okay, but I can't take Zeus with me."

"Is Carina in?" I'd just passed the office, so I stopped walking in case I really did have to pop in and get the cat.

"No, and I don't know when she'll be back."

"What about Julian?"

He sighed, loudly. "Yes, but you don't ex——"

"He's a good guy. He'll be fine with it. Look, I'll call him and ask. Okay?" I probably could take Zeus to the police station with me, but Bellamy might not appreciate it.

"Fine, but you owe me."

"I'll add it to my tab. Thank you, Vinegar!"

He grumbled something, which I couldn't make out, and then said, "Goodbye."

I called Julian, confirmed he was fine with having the cat in his office for an hour, and texted Finn, telling him to move Zeus to there. And that was that.

I hurried along the main street until I reached the café. It was open again. That must be a relief for Anna. I didn't have time to go in, but I'd come back and talk to her this afternoon. Unfortunately, there was no sign of that sleazy ghost. Maybe Charles had had some luck discovering who he was. If I didn't run into the young ghost at the station, I'd call him to me when I was in my car, and we could chat on the way back to the office.

Daisy was waiting in the laneway near my place, her yellow paintwork shiny and clean. Since Bellamy had given Joyless's brother a warning, I'd had no more problems with vandalism, but sometimes, the tension was still there in the moment before I turned the corner and saw her.

There wasn't much traffic on the way to the station, so it didn't take long. PC Adams was manning the front counter. "Hey, Avery. How's things?"

"Okay, busy. How about you?"

"Same." She laughed. "So, I don't want to sound needy, but you haven't baked a tart for a while." Her eyebrows waggled.

I chuckled. "Well, I'll have to rectify that next time I come in." Although, the way things had been going, I might end up back here again tomorrow. "Hmm, what about if I promise to have one here sometime in the next two weeks?"

"Works for me. So, you're here to see the sergeant, I take it."

"You betcha."

She pressed the button to unlock the security door, and it buzzed. "Thanks, PC Adams. Wish me luck." I had no idea why he'd called me here, and there were too many reasons to choose from, half of them bad.

"Luck."

I didn't spy Fox as I walked down the hallway to the main office area. There was no need to see him in secret any more, now that we could talk in front of Bellamy. PC Patel said hello as I passed his desk. "Hi, PC Patel. Busy day?"

He smiled. "Always. Arrested a naked man at the bakery this morning."

"Lucky you!" I laughed.

He gave a wry grin. "You could say that…."

I kept moving and ignored the nerves sloshing around my belly. Surely I wasn't in trouble for anything. When I thought back to the last couple of days, there was nothing I'd done that stood out, unless Mrs Crabby complained about the noise this morning. If that's all it was, then I could relax. I knocked on Bellamy's door.

"Come in."

Charles sat on one of the visitor seats, and Fox stood next to Bellamy's chair. "Hi, Sergeant. So, I hope I'm not in trouble."

His smile spoke of amusement. "Why? Is there something you should be in trouble for?"

I took the seat next to Charles. "No, but I can't work out why you called me in."

"Hello to you, too, Avery." Charles gave me an irritated look.

I turned to him. "Sorry. Hello, Charles." Old habits died hard. It was weird that I could be myself in front of Bellamy. Not that he wasn't giving me a weird look right now. He must be taking a while to really get used to it. I looked at Bellamy. "Charles is sitting there, and Sergeant Fox is standing next to you, on your left."

Bellamy looked to his left, then to the space Charles was, and back to me. He shook his head. "If you say so." If only there was some way I could help him see my friends. I chuckled to myself. Spoken like a true crazy person.

"I know it's hard to get your head around. My own family thinks I'm bonkers. Anyway, I have a few things I need to do today, so…." I hated being rude, but I wanted to get to those interviews for Zeus and put that locket in the paper. Whoever had lost it had obviously lost it a while ago, but for some reason, my psyche was telling me to hurry up and find them. Strange, but I wasn't going to question it because there was no answer there, and I had better things to do.

"Ah, yes. Sorry. The results for the coffee came back, and they were positive for cyanide. We found a small container of it in the café storeroom with Ms Stick's fingerprints on it, and there was some in the almond milk container. We've formally arrested and charged Joy Stick with murder."

Now would be a very bad time to laugh at her name. I bit the inside of my cheek. Charles didn't laugh, but that was probably because he'd died before video games existed. Now for the appropriate response. "Oh, wow. What a horrible way to die. I wondered if maybe he'd had a heart attack, but he did say his coffee tasted acidic."

"When did the victim say that?"

"After he died. His ghost said it when I asked."

He leaned forward and dropped his hands on the tabletop. "Why didn't you tell us?"

"Well, I couldn't exactly tell you when PC Patel was there."

"You could've called me afterwards."

He made a good point, but…. "I didn't want to confuse your investigation."

His eyes bugged wide. "That's never stopped you before."

Another good point. "Yes, well, I was going to tell you when you received your initial test results. I figured I'd step in if and when you needed me to. So it sounds like this confirms what the lab found. I appreciate you calling me in to update me, though. Thank you." I smiled but thought better of it when I saw the shady expression on Bellamy's face, not to mention that Charles was rolling his eyes. "Hang on. You didn't call me out of the goodness of your heart, did you?"

He cleared his throat and smoothed down the front of his shirt. "I knew you wanted to be updated, but something else came up when I was interviewing Miss Stick. She pleaded her innocence"—which we both knew meant nothing—"but she mentioned that either you were crazy or you could see ghosts. She told me about the conversation you had with her deceased ex-boyfriend's ghost. She also asked me to ask you if you could see her today. I wanted to talk to you and find out what else you knew, and then you can visit her in the cells."

Right, so she swore she was innocent, and even though the physical evidence pointed to her, there was that ghost. And why did she want to see me? Did she want to threaten me or make fun of me? It would be a stupid reason to want to see me, but this was Joyless we were talking about.

In any case, if I was going to tell Bellamy everything the ex said, it was going to add to her looking guilty. "But you know she owed her ex money." I'd put that in my statement since that conversation happened while he was still alive. "After he died, he told me she'd threatened him while they were together and after they broke up." I recounted what he'd said as close to word for word as I could get. "There was another ghost. A shady-looking older man. He didn't realise I could see him, and after the victim died, he said his boss would be happy."

"You're doing well, Avery." Charles smiled.

"Thanks, Charles." At least I had a support person… ghost.

"Okay, so she's not exactly a pleasant person when she's angry."

My eyebrows leapt to the ceiling. "Not just when she's angry. You saw what she did to me with that stupid Facebook post. Any time she doesn't get what she wants, or she feels threatened, she lashes out. She's one of the most horrible people I've ever met." And that was saying something. "She's had me in her sights since the day I got here. When I first bought coffee for everyone at work, she ripped me off on purpose. I don't know what I did, but she hates me." Yikes. I hadn't meant to let it all out. Maybe it was about time I said what was really on my mind. Even though I might look petty, I felt better for having said it.

He blinked, cleared his throat, and rubbed the back of his neck. Not much flustered the sergeant, but apparently talking about women feuding did, especially when one of those women was speaking passionately. He probably thought I was being silly and making a tsunami out of a ripple, but it was never that easy when you were living with bullying. It always made me fume when you told someone about things like this, and they immediately assumed you were overreacting. It was one of my pet hates. "So… you wouldn't make something up to make her look worse, would you?"

My mouth dropped open. "You must be kidding. Please tell me you're joking." He had the decency to blush. "Why would

I? There's already physical evidence that could put her away for a long time. Why would I bother?"

"To stick the boot in?"

I shook my head and tried to ignore the burning in my chest at the injustice that he would think me capable. "I also just mentioned that strange ghost, which might lead to other information proving her innocence." I let air whoosh loudly out of my nostrils. "I'm insulted right now. I can't believe you'd think that of me after everything you've seen. When have I ever given you the impression that I'd lie to get back at someone?" Had I trusted the wrong person with my secret? Regret punched me in the gut, adrenaline racing through my bloodstream as memories of my parents and Brad and what they'd put me through surfaced. This was another reminder of why I couldn't tell any of my friends. I couldn't truly trust anyone. At least I could avoid Bellamy, and even if he didn't like me, I couldn't see him telling everyone what I'd told him in confidence.

"I'm sorry I had to say that, but I wanted to be sure. It would have been an oversight for me not to have asked. We also have motive with her not wanting to repay the money, and we can add the fact that she's hurt since he broke up with her and is now dating someone else. I also can't fathom how a third party could know when Alan was going to be at the café and put poison in the almond milk at the precise time. I agree that it looks like we have a firm case against Miss Stick, but because she's a valued member of our community"—I coughed at that—"I think we should explore all avenues. So, tell me about this other ghost. Do you know his name? Have you ever seen him before?"

"It's okay, Avery. Just take a couple of deep breaths. Bellamy's not against you." Charles tried to rest a hand on my arm, but it fell through. I jerked at the pinch of cold. He meant well, but it would take more than some kind words to chase away the anger that had taken residence in my body.

I struggled to keep my voice calm and even. Being able to walk it off for ten minutes would've been ideal. "No and no. And, as much as I dislike Joy, if she is innocent, I would hate for the real killer to get away. Which reminds me. Can you excuse me for one second, Sergeant?"

His forehead wrinkled. "Ah, okay, Miss Winters."

I angled my body towards Charles. "Did you find anything out about our large friend?"

"I asked around about him, but I'm still waiting on a name. A couple of the local ghosts had seen him hanging around before, but none of them knew him. One ghost did see him talking to another ghost he knew, so he's finding out for me from them. And before you ask when they're getting back to me, I have no idea. He might think he's rushing back to me, but it's actually two weeks in your time."

I sighed. Why was nothing ever simple? "Okay. Can you let me know as soon as you know?" *Please don't take two weeks.*

"Yep."

I shifted to face Bellamy. "Charles is working on discovering who it is. He has a lead, but he's waiting for a name. As soon as I find that out, I'll let you know, and I'll chase it up too. I've been hoping to run into the ghost so I can ask him some questions; although I'm not sure how much he'll help me." Something else crossed my mind. "Um, can we all"—I moved my gaze from Bellamy to Fox to Charles—"not let it be known that Sergeant Bellamy knows about my ability? I have a feeling that whoever is behind the murder—providing it's not Joy— wouldn't be too happy if they knew I had an inkling there was something else going on, which would only be made worse if they thought I had the ear of the local police sergeant. We have to remember that this living person can talk to the dead, too, so they already know I can see ghosts because their little messenger spirit would've told them."

Sergeant Fox said, "Of course, Miss Winters," while Bellamy nodded, and Charles said, "Of course."

Now that was settled, I had a question for Bellamy. "Since this might not be a clear-cut case, did you ask Alan's friends, girlfriend, family, and co-workers if he had any enemies?"

Bellamy cocked his head to the side and folded his arms. "Miss Winters, of course. It was one of the first questions we asked."

I waited for him to elaborate, but it seemed as if there was nothing to say, or he was hiding something. "Sergeant Bellamy, are you going to expand on that?"

He peered at me, maybe thinking. Eventually, he said, "I'll reserve judgement on that until after you see Miss Stick. I'll be here waiting when you return." He stood and opened his door. "Patel, can you take Miss Winters to see Miss Stick?"

Patel jumped up. "On it, Sergeant."

I silently screamed in my head. Even when she was locked up, I still couldn't avoid her. I stood and followed Patel through a security door with a nine-digit code.

"Are you and Miss Stick good friends, then?"

I choked on my own saliva and coughed. "Not at all. She hates me. She wanted to see me, and I have no idea why. Maybe she wants to take out some frustration?"

Patel chuckled. "Ah, okay." We ended up in a room that had a table and three chairs. The door had a glass panel with reinforcing wire criss-crossing inside it. Must be a security window. "Wait here, and I'll bring her in."

I was too nervous to sit. She might even want to hit me. I stood with my back to the wall, hands by my sides ready to move.

But when Patel brought her in and made her sit on the

other side of the table from where I stood, she had her hands cuffed in front of her. His voice was all authority when he said, "Behave. I'll be outside there, watching. You do anything, and it will be added to your charges." Wow, had he taken me seriously before when I said how much she disliked me? He gave me a nod as he left. "If you need anything, yell out. I'll be just outside." Sure enough, when he left the room and shut the door, he went no further than that. He stood in the hallway watching us. That made me feel marginally better, but my heart was still working away at a higher rate than normal.

I pretended she was someone I didn't know, and I was interviewing her for the paper. "So, why did you want to see me?" As long as I kept the fear out of my voice, she should stay calm, kind of like when a vicious animal was stalking you —if you didn't smell like fear, and you didn't run, they might decide to leave you alone.

Her eyes watched me intently. Her mouth puckered as if she'd just tasted something gross. Annoyance flashed across her face, and she sat up straight, regally, as if she was wearing a ballgown and crown rather than torn jeans, a boring, grey sweatshirt, and bracelets care of His Majesty. "You're gonna help me get out of here."

"What? Are you asking me to break you out of jail?"

She rolled her eyes. "No, stupid. You're going to prove my innocence by finding whoever really killed Alan."

I stood straighter and folded my arms. "Why in Hades would I help you? You hate me. You've made my life as hard as possible since I arrived here. Besides, don't you think I'm crazy?"

She glanced down at her handcuffs, her smug expression faltering. Remembering you were in jail would do that to a person. When she looked back up at me, reluctance had replaced the smug expression. She sniffed in what appeared to be annoyance. "I don't think you're crazy any more. Not after you said all those things. Only Alan knew them. I didn't believe in that stuff before, but I'm not an idiot. If you'd known that stuff earlier, you probably would've used it against me. I believe that Alan told you after he died."

It had cost her to say it, and I wasn't going to deny the satisfaction unfurling inside me. Still, I wasn't going to give in without making my point. "Okay, so you don't think I'm crazy. Great. But you still hate me for no reason. So why would I help you?"

The self-satisfied expression was back. She sure didn't know how asking for help worked. "You can't help yourself. You love to do the right thing, Miss Goody Two Shoes. You even risk your life for people you don't know, just to get to the truth." She rolled her eyes like I was queen of the morons. "I don't know why you bother, but you do, and so you're going to help me."

She wasn't wrong in her assessment—she wasn't as dumb as I'd thought, which made her eviler than I'd assumed. She didn't treat people badly out of ignorance. It was because she was just a horrible person, which I kind of knew anyway. But if she thought I'd help her because it was an uncontrollable urge, she'd just poked the drop bear. This nice person also had a stubborn side. It's what got me out of my rut and to England. It's what got me to the end of cases that were hard to solve. I loved a challenge.

"No." It was my turn to wear a smug smile. *Put that in your pipe and smoke it.* Yes, I'd already decided it was the right thing to do, that there was enough doubt that I was going to get involved; however, she didn't need to know that... yet. Two could play at being evil.

Her eyes widened, and she leaned back. *Surprise!* "You can't say no."

I laughed. "Why not?"

She stared, and her mouth worked before shutting. It would be interesting to see how long it took before she realised she'd need to ask nicely and apologise for treating me like crap previously.

Although, judging by the sly expression that stole over her face, she wasn't about to do any of that. "I'll tell Finn all about you talking to ghosts. I know how much he loves those kinds of people."

My stomach hit the floor. I did my best to keep the horror from showing on my face. I swallowed. She really had hit me where it hurt, but then again, I wasn't going to give in to a bully. Never again. I'd let Bellamy know what she was planning, and if he could put in a good word with Finn and I just kept denying everything, hopefully he'd believe me. It was a chance I'd have to take.

My face relaxed into a serene expression, and I told myself I believed what I was about to say. *Nothing can hurt me*. "I don't care. I'll just deny everything. Who do you think he'll believe—a murderer or his workmate?" She scowled. "Look, I've got stuff to do. In fact, I'm having lunch with Vinegar. I'm sure we'll talk about you since it's such big news in town at the moment." Was I being too mean? Maybe, but she deserved a bit of what she doled out. I walked to the door and opened it. "When you're ready to ask nicely, let Sergeant Bellamy know, and maybe I'll come back. See ya."

She jumped to her feet. She wasn't exactly shouting, but it was close. "But you can't! I'll ruin you worse than I already have. Just wait!"

"Enjoy prison. You'll fit right in." I strode out, and PC Patel walked in and ushered her out and down the hallway.

"You'll regret this," she called angrily over her shoulder.

I did feel guilty, but giving her what she demanded

wouldn't teach her anything at all. Getting her own way when she was little was possibly one reason she ended up being a total piece of poo. Besides, I'd be working on her case in the background. I'd just have to make sure Sergeant Bellamy took all the credit; although, when she finally got out of jail—providing she was innocent—she'd be gunning for me. At least I had time to figure it out, and what if she had played a part in Alan's murder? I didn't really believe that, but I'd be stupid not to consider it.

It was time to try and find more evidence and get to the facts. If she was innocent and got released, I'd have to deal with that when it happened. I'd figure it all out. I always did.

CHAPTER 6

I sat at the computer and pressed Send on the small piece with a photo of the locket I'd found that would go on the Lost and Found page. There. I'd already sent off the Manesbury Fair article as well. I looked at the time. 2:57 p.m. The first interview for Zeus's prospective new family would be here in three minutes. I looked at the cutie, who was asleep in his cat bed next to my chair.

Carina was out, but Finn was here because I'd asked him to stay to give a second opinion on the prospective adopters. I knew some people took in dogs or cats just so they could be cruel to them. There was no way I wanted someone like that getting hold of Zeus.

"He's so cute." Erin, the ghost child who haunted the office, sat next to him and tried to pat him. "I wish I was alive so I could feel his soft fur." Zeus shivered but didn't wake. I gave Erin a sad smile because I couldn't exactly say anything.

Finn stopped typing and peered at me. "Are you okay? You look kind of sad looking at the cat like that."

I met his gaze. "I'm going to miss him, and I want to make

sure he goes to a good home. What if we make a mistake and the person who takes him treats him badly, or what if they're careless and he gets onto the road and gets squashed?"

He smiled. "Hey, catastrophizer, it's going to be okay."

"Seriously, we can't give him to just anyone. You should look up how many pets are abused each year or dumped. The figures are disturbing. People disappoint me sometimes."

Oops, I'd upset Erin, who stared up at me with huge doe eyes. "Oh no. Why can't you take him?" Why did everyone have to ask me that?

I knew I couldn't answer her to her face, so I redirected it to Finn. "If I could take him, I totally would. Mrs Crabby would kick me out. You know that. I've fallen for Zeus. He's the biggest sweetie. Didn't you enjoy having him around?"

Erin frowned. "Oh, I'm sorry, Avery." Having two conversations at once was dangerous. I was bound to say the wrong thing and have Finn think I'd totally lost the plot.

"Of course I enjoyed having him around. He's adorable and great to snuggle up to." I was not going to get jealous of a cat. Nope. "But cat sitting is very different to owning and being responsible for another life 24/7."

"Cats pretty much look after themselves once you've fed and watered them. And changed their litter." Hmm, I wasn't really selling this very well.

"And walked them. Zeus is a special cat. He's more like a dog. That woman was right—he needs lots of attention, and I don't know that I can give him as much as he deserves." He tilted his head to the side and gave me an apologetic look.

I blew out a breath. "I'm sorry. I don't want to force him on you. I just thought you'd make a good dad for Zeus. Hopefully someone who comes in this arvo will be suitable."

Knock, knock. I started and jerked around to look at the door. The first person was here. I stood and opened the door.

A skinny man in his thirties stood there. His hair was short, his skin pale, and his white T-shirt stained with what looked like tomato sauce. Each of his hands was held by a child. One of the girls looked to be about four, the other six or seven. "Hi. I'm here about the cat. It's free, right?"

"Um, yes, and he comes with some food, bed, and other things. Please come in."

The girls dropped his hands and hurried to where Zeus slept. The eldest girl dropped to the ground and poked Zeus in the stomach. "Wake up, cat!"

"Um, please be gentle with him." The girl didn't even look at me.

"Did you hear the lady, Lizzy?" She didn't acknowledge her father, either, and poked Zeus again. Zeus opened his eyes, stretched, and stood. He seemed to be assessing the small person in front of him. He decided he didn't trust her—at least that was my take on it—and jumped onto my table, stood on his hind legs, and put his paws on my chest. I picked him up.

"It's okay, buddy."

The father eyed Zeus. "That's the cat? Doesn't seem so friendly. Your article said he was affectionate."

"That's only for people who are nice to him. I guess he doesn't like to be poked." I moved my gaze to the little girl. She stuck her tongue out at me.

Hmm, this was devolving.

Finn stood and came over, thank God. He held out his hand to the guy. "I'm Finn. Nice to meet you…?"

"Roger. Pleased to meet you."

Finn smiled. "Right, so we have a few questions for everyone who comes to see Zeus. Do you have any other pets?"

"Some chickens out the back." He side-eyed Zeus. "He won't eat them, will he?"

I shrugged. "Maybe. I don't know."

The little girl who'd poked Zeus grabbed his tail and pulled. I turned with him in my arms, yanking it out of her grasp. Zeus growled. "I'm sorry, sweetie. It's okay." I stroked his back, trying to calm him. I was probably super lucky he hadn't scratched the stuffing out of me when his tail was pulled. "I'm sorry, but you're not suitable. Zeus needs to be with a family with older children. The last owner said he once almost scratched her niece's eye out. I should've put that in the ad."

The guy swore. "You've got to be joking me. I drove fifteen minutes to come down here. Waste of time. Stupid cat anyway. It can't even defend itself." He looked at his brats. Okay, to be fair, only one of them had shown themselves to be a brat, but still, give the other one some time. "Come on, girls." He held his hands out for them. Thankfully, they grasped them without complaint, and they left.

I kissed the top of Zeus's head. "You just dodged two bullets there, bud. I'm sure the next people will be better."

Finn scratched his head and stared at the empty hallway before closing the door and turning to me. "Hmm, you weren't wrong, but that was probably a fluke. The next people will be nice. You'll see."

"Hmm, yes, we can hope."

We waited another twenty minutes for the next people, a young, rich couple. She wore Chanel earrings and carried an Yves St Laurent bag. Her nails were done to perfection—French polish—and her hair was styled, not one strand out of place. His black leather shoes shone, and his blue shirt was pressed, the sleeves rolled to halfway up his forearms. He wore a Rolex, and a thin gold chain glittered around his neck through the gap in his shirt. They carried themselves with an air of superiority.

As soon as they walked through the door, the guy sauntered across the room and shook Finn's hand. Of course he did. I resisted temptation and did not roll my eyes. I gave Zeus an "I don't know about this" look instead.

"Are you the guy selling the cat?"

His girlfriend, or whoever she was, had found Zeus curled in his bed. "Oh, he's adorable." At least she seemed okay. She cocked her head to the side as she regarded him. "I'm not sure if he's the right colour, though." She looked over at her partner. "What do you think, darling?"

Rolex guy came over and crouched near Zeus. "I think he'll go with the couch and the rug. Maybe he could be a bit darker, but I think it'll be fine." He patted Zeus. "He's nice and soft. Have a pat." *Could be a bit darker*? They wanted him as an accessory?

She giggled. "No, I don't think so. Then I'd have to wash my hands." She glanced around. "I don't see any sink and soap around here. Besides, he's more for you than me. You'll be feeding him and cleaning his litter." Her mouth made a small O. "Oh, do you think we could teach him to use the toilet? He would have his own. The less we have to do for him, the better."

Rolex guy stood and looked at her. "You make a good point about the toilet. But feeding him might be an issue. You won't do it when I'm away for work. And we can't not have him eating for a week at a time." My eyes bugged out, and I threw a horrified look at Finn. His mouth had dropped open. *Yep, Vinegar, listen to them, and listen well.* I figured it was going to be hard to find someone for Zeus, but this was ridiculous.

She waved her perfectly manicured hand. "I'll pay someone to come feed him."

I kept staring at Finn, who'd moved his incredulous stare to the couple. I raised one brow as if to say "see, I told you there were lots of nutters around." He saw me and shook his head, looked at them, then me again.

Before the couple could say they wanted him, I said, "I'm sorry. I've just decided that I'm going to adopt him." Okay, so I wasn't, but I couldn't think of another reason to give them. They looked like the kind of people who wouldn't take no easily.

The guy looked at me, then turned to Finn. "What the hell, mate? I hope you haven't wasted our time."

Finn shrugged. "We've been interviewing people all day. We want to make sure he goes to the right home, but he needs someone who will give him lots of affection. I can't see that your partner will, and you're too busy with whatever important job you have." He was putting it all back on them, which was good. They could see he meant business and hopefully wouldn't argue.

The woman pursed her lips. "Well, this has been inconvenient. I suppose it's all for the better because he's not quite the right colour. Come on, darling. Let's go."

Thankfully they left without further argument. I shut the door after them and shuddered. My heart fell for the poor cat that finally made the cut. I looked at Finn. "I received a couple more emails this afternoon. I'll call them and get them to come in."

"Yeah. If they can't come in today, that's fine. I can take him one more night."

I smiled. "Thanks. And thanks for backing me up. Honestly, there are some weirdos out there, and they're not fit to have a pet."

"I hate saying it, Lightning, but you were right."

My smile morphed into a grin. "I hate to be right about

this, but yeah. Also, I'm often right, Vinegar. You should know that by now."

"I'm pleading the fifth."

I laughed. "Sorry to break it to you, but we're not in the US."

He picked up Zeus and gave him a cuddle. The cat snuggled under his chin. "You're the perfect colour, little boy. Forget what those morons said. They know nothing." Finn's gaze found mine. "Look how adorable he is."

I knew he was trying to change the subject, but I'd let him get away with it this time because he was bonding with Zeus. Hopefully I'd be right about him being the best person other than me to adopt the cat. If I gave him enough kitty rope, he might just be tangled up in it too much to escape before he knew what happened. "Yes, Vinegar. He's totally adorable."

After making appointments to meet with the other prospective adopters and lining up another article interview, I drove home, glancing at the café as I passed. That ghost wasn't there and probably never would be. Disappointment sat heavily in my gut. What if Charles couldn't locate him? It was time I made more of an effort to research who this guy was. Maybe I should start with mug shots from the 1920s to the 1950s. Bellamy would likely give me access to that information, although sifting through those records was going to be a huge job. And he could be from anywhere, although I'd assumed that he was from around here somewhere; otherwise, why was he hanging around? It seemed from the ghosts I'd met that they didn't go far from where their home had been when they died.

Finn had driven to work today, and since I left first, I

snagged the premium spot, which would normally make me smile—it had become a bit of a game between us—but I wasn't in the mood. It was more because of Zeus than Joyless. What if we couldn't find him a good home? Could I afford to move? I'd miss living near Meg and Finn, but I had some savings, and now I had a steady income, I could afford to spend an extra twenty or thirty pounds a week on accommodation. It was more a matter of finding something in my price range within a fifteen-minute drive of Manesbury. I didn't want a long commute, not to mention petrol costs.

When I let myself in downstairs, I tripped and slapped the wall. *Noooooo!* I shut the door quietly and started up the stairs, my back tingling with anticipation. There was no way Mrs Crabby was going to let that slide.

But I made it to my door with no issues.

Hmm, maybe she was out or stuck on the loo. I chuckled. I could just see her trying to finish in a hurry and not being able to, and the anger on her face. I hurriedly shut my door and locked it behind me. I'd made it in safe and sound.

"Hey, Avery."

I jumped and turned around. "Oh my God, Ev. How many times do I have to tell you not to surprise me? Call to me from outside or maybe from the bedroom."

She laughed. "But it's so much fun to scare you. Don't you want me to be happy?" She gave me a cheesy grin.

"Yes, but not at my expense. Sheesh."

"So, what have you been up to the last couple of days?" She sat her ghostly self on the couch, and I sat next to her.

"There's been another murder, and I've got to find a home for a cat."

She sat forward. "Ooh, so did the dead person ask you to help their cat?"

"Oh, no, they're not related." I blinked, then stared. My heartbeat thudded in my ears.

"What's wrong?" Everly's forehead wrinkled, and she played with the locket peeking through her shirt.

I swallowed. "Does that locket have initials on the back?"

"Yeah, why?"

I'd managed to put my bag on the dining table before she'd surprised me, so I jumped up and went to it. I found the locket and returned to the couch. I didn't bother sitting down because the nervous energy made me want to stand and shift from foot to foot. I held the silver-coloured locket in front of her face, and it swung in small movements from side to side. "Is this yours?" I turned it around so she could see all of it; then I opened it and showed her the brown, almost unrecognisable photo inside.

She sucked in a breath, even though she didn't breathe. It still bothered me that ghosts did that, but anyway. She held her hand out to touch it but went through. Her head tilted up, watery eyes regarding me. "Yes, it's mine. I was wearing it the day I died. W-where did you find it?" That was the most information she'd given me about her murder. We'd only spoken about it once before, and she'd seemed reluctant to provide any information. I'd assumed it was because she didn't want to relive it, but maybe she'd also blocked a lot of it out. And if her brain had chosen to protect her from that trauma, I couldn't blame it.

I stared at the locket and chain in my hand. This could be evidence, and I'd moved it and washed it. I'd have to give it to Bellamy, admit what a silly thing I'd done, and show him where I found it. "At the edge of the forest, about half-an-hour's walk from here."

Her throat bobbed with a swallow. Silence was what she gave me for at least a minute. This must be such a shock for her, even though she was wearing the ghostly form of it around her neck. Did it bring back bad memories or good? By the way she tugged at the ghostly version and the lost look in her eyes as she stared at the real locket, they were probably bad.

"Are you okay?"

Her head snapped up, her eyes meeting mine. "What are you going to do with it?"

"Seeing as how it's yours and you were murdered, I'm passing it onto the police. It's evidence. But I stupidly washed it, so now any DNA would be long gone." What a waste of time me finding it was now. Had I inadvertently prevented her murder from ever being solved? *Way to stuff it up, Avery.*

Her fingers curled around the locket and trembled. "Do you have to?"

"Yes. It's the responsible thing to do." And now I didn't have to worry about anyone seeing it in the paper and claiming it. Chances were that her family weren't even alive any more. She never mentioned them. Was the murderer still alive and around here?

She stood. "I'm going to go sit in the bedroom. Is that okay? I need time to process, and I'd rather do it here where I feel safe."

"Of course! This is your home more than it is mine. You don't even have to ask, Ev. I'm so sorry I can't hug you." I rubbed my forehead where a headache was starting. "If you need company, let me know."

Her eyes brimmed with tears. She nodded, turned, and disappeared into the bedroom.

I sat back on the couch and stared unseeing at the wall. I'd call Bellamy tomorrow because he was probably in bed, and no one could do anything tonight. My head sunk into my palms. Why did I wash it? So stupid, but then again, the markings on the locket wouldn't have been visible if I hadn't. Had she been killed where I found the locket? Was her body buried nearby? At least Bellamy would now believe me when I told him where I found it. My discovery was likely to start a burst of activity—at least I hoped it did.

A voice came from outside the front door. "Avery, it's Charles."

I smiled. At least someone respected that I hated surprises. "Come in!"

He slid through the door, and I shuddered. It was something I still hadn't adapted to, kind of like rubbing my dry hand against a dry beach towel. It gave me the icks and probably always would.

"Please tell me you have some good news." The only good thing that had happened today was that Mrs Crabby hadn't attacked me for making noise this afternoon.

Charles smiled and sat next to me. "I do. I've found out that ghost's name and where he hangs out."

"Wow, that's awesome. Thank you! How did you manage that?" As much as I didn't care about Joyless, I did love the truth, and maybe, just maybe, if she was innocent and I helped her get out of jail, she might think twice before being a total screaming haemorrhoid. And if Manesbury knew I'd helped her get out of jail, it would be a massive point to me. It might improve my public image. So maybe I wouldn't let Bellamy take all the credit if she was innocent, but I wouldn't be telling her that any time soon. I'd let her stew in her misery for a while.

"Mrs Shillington, a Manesbury ghost, was across the road when Alan was murdered. She heard I was asking around about that gangster-looking guy. Her husband borrowed money from a gang in Exmouth, back in the 1940s. That man used to come and collect the repayments. Once, when he didn't have the full amount for that month, the guy beat him badly. His name is Ironfist McTavish, real name Donald Arthur McTavish. He frequents a pool hall in Cramptonbury with a few of his old gang members. I popped in for a look and found him, but I didn't let on who I was or what I was doing. I got kicked out for being underaged."

My forehead scrunched. "What? You're a ghost. Does it matter? Also, how did they even do that?"

He frowned. "I might've existed for way more years than a child, but other ghosts don't see it that way. They treat me like a child." Which he still kind of was. A smart child who'd seen a lot, but his brain still worked like a child's in some ways. He was a quick thinker but still naïve about many things.

"And how did they kick you out if they can't touch you?"

"There were four criminals, including the guy you're after. They surrounded me and combined their energies. They were giving off waves of… badness, and it made me scared. It felt like when my dad took his belt off and came at me. It's hard to explain how I know, but they were more powerful than normal ghosts. I didn't think twice—I just left." His cheeks pinkened.

"Hey, don't be embarrassed about that. That's a normal response to something like that, and I'd rather you were safe than not. You've done something fantastic, Charles, and there was no way I would've been able to find him without you." I smiled and lifted my hand to rub his back, but then I remembered and dropped my arm. I sighed instead.

He fidgeted his hands in his lap. "I'm sorry I couldn't find out who he was working for."

I cocked my head to the side and peered at him. "That's fine. You need to leave something for me to do." I winked.

He risked a small smile. "Thanks, Avery."

"No, thank you. You've saved the day."

"I have?" He didn't sound sure at all.

I grinned. "Yes, totally." Then I told him all about my day and every failure. Thankfully, by the time he left, he was smiling. And that was my cue to cook dinner and wonder what Bellamy would say when I brought Everly's locket in. I knew the ghost wasn't keen on me restarting an investigation, but it was the right thing to do. Her murderer could still be alive, and who knew if he or she had killed since or would again?

Maybe getting to the bottom of what happened to Everly would help more than just her. I hated that it was opening old wounds, but sometimes the price for justice was high. Except this time, I wouldn't be the one paying it. Did I hate myself right now for needing to pursue it? Yes. But I couldn't change who I was. I would always do the right thing, even if it hurt. And this time, it was going to hurt someone I cared about. I crossed my fingers that she'd understand in time because losing her friendship would break my heart.

CHAPTER 7

The morning came, and my first port of call was the office, so I stopped in at the café to grab my coffee, safe in the knowledge that Joyless wouldn't be there. I figured Anna could do with the support, and I hadn't spoken to her since it happened. Besides, my day was going to be crazy busy, and a large cappuccino to jumpstart me was just what I needed.

When I walked in, there was one lady waiting for a beverage, which meant it was quiet for a weekday morning. The pastries under glass were usually half gone by now, but the cabinet was almost full. I didn't make a habit of buying food because I was always trying to save a pound, but I couldn't bear to see her lose money from something that was out of her control. Besides, I was sure that Carina would love a pastry, and I needed to do something to thank Finn for looking after Zeus. By the time Anna had handed the woman's coffee over and looked at me, I knew what I'd order.

"Avery, hey. How are you?" Her just-longer-than-shoulder-length brown hair was down today. Her usually bright smile was dimmed.

"I'm fine, but more importantly, how are you holding up?"

"I don't know. Hanging on, I suppose. I just can't believe Joy would poison someone… in my shop." She rubbed her forehead. "I've hardly slept since it happened. How did I not see how unhinged she was? How could she do something like that? And I'm so sorry you were here to see the poor man die." She took a deep breath and clutched her stomach. Was she going to have an anxiety attack?

"Are you okay? Do you need to sit down?"

"No, no. I'm okay. I just…."

I couldn't take it any longer. I might not be able to properly comfort my ghostly friends, but I sure as Hades could hug my living ones. I hurried behind the counter and gave her a huge hug. "If you need any help, let me know. I can come in and help with the morning rush. I'll just make my *Manesbury Daily* appointments later."

"Thank you, Avery, but it's okay. It hasn't exactly been busy since we reopened yesterday afternoon." She sniffled and leaned out of my hug.

I went back to the customer side of the counter. "It'll pick up again. Don't worry. And if you need my help when that happens, sing out."

"Thanks. I appreciate it, but it won't be a problem. I'm going to have to find someone else to fill Joy's spot. It's not like she's on holidays. She might be back in a few months or years. Who knows?" She wiped her hands down her apron. "From what the police said, it's an open-and-shut case, but what do you think? You were here. Is she guilty? You seem to have a knack for this stuff."

I didn't want to give her false hope, and was that a twinge of compassion that she was going to lose her job? If they released her soon, maybe the spot wouldn't be filled. I hated my sense of fairness coming out right now and telling me that I should figure out who really killed Alan ASAP because if it wasn't Joy, she deserved to be free and have her old job back. Grrrr. "Um, I don't know. It looks like she did it, but from what Sergeant Bellamy told me, they're still interviewing Alan's friends and family. As you know, Joy and I don't really get along. She's… disliked me since I arrived, but if she is innocent, I'll do whatever I can to help." That was as much as I could say without giving anything else away.

Anna's lips curled up slightly. "Thank you, Avery. You're a good egg. Now, what can I get for you?"

"A large cappuccino and three chocolate eclairs. I think my workmates could do with some carbs this morning."

"Your *workmates*, huh?" She grinned.

"Ahem, yes."

When she was done, she thanked me again and asked me to keep her up to date if anything changed with Joy. I promised I would, and then I made my way into the office. At the top of the stairs, before I could drop off my sugary spoils, Julian came down the hallway. "Winters, just the person I wanted to see."

"Morning. What can I do for you? Is it about the cat?" Was he reneging on us having Zeus in the office already?

"No. But how is the little fur ball?"

"He's good. I have two more people coming in today to see if they're suitable to adopt him."

He tapped his hand against his thigh a few times. "Good luck. Anyway, I wanted to ask you about that locket you put in the lost and found section."

"Oh, why?" The hairs on the back of my neck stood up. What was he asking about that for? Had someone called?

"We've had a call about it from Mrs Collins, your landlady.

As you know, we didn't show the back and asked that anyone calling tell us what was engraved on there. She said it was EC —her daughter's initials, apparently. She said she gave it to her for her sixteenth birthday. Are those initials right because I can't remember?"

My stomach clear fell through the floor as everything clicked into place in my brain. Everly was Mrs Crabby's daughter? Holy moly! It made sense. Was that why Mrs Collins had turned into Mrs Crabby? And was that why she'd been reluctant to lease the flat upstairs out… because her daughter had lived there? "Um…." And now I'd have to tread carefully because I couldn't give it back to Mrs Crabby, but would it look sus if I said I knew about the murder? "Yes, those are the initials. But now that I know who it belonged to, I'm going to have to hand it over to the police. I heard her daughter had disappeared and was considered deceased. Isn't that right?"

He rubbed his chin. "Yes, she was. Right." He went back to tapping his thigh as he spun that around his brain. "Okay, then. I'll tell her that we're going to have to hand it over to the police as evidence, and that she can have it back soon. How's that?"

"Sounds good to me. Thanks."

"No. Thank you. Maybe they'll reopen the case into her disappearance. I remember they found her bloody cardigan near her house, but there was no sign of the body. Very sad case."

"Very sad." Wow, okay, now my sympathy metre went off the charts for the old lady. How could I be annoyed with her, knowing why she was so cranky? Unless she'd always been like that. I'd have to talk to Everly about it, now the secret of who they were to each other was out. Hmm, but why hadn't Everly ever said anything about Mrs Crabby being her mum? I blew out a breath.

"Are you okay, Winters?"

"Yes, I'm fine. Just feeling bad for Mrs Collins. Anyway, I'd better get to it. I have a lot on today."

"Good-oh. See you later." His feet tapped a lively staccato as he continued down the stairs and out the front door.

I took a few moments to compose myself, then opened the office door, which was probably shut because Zeus was inside. Carina and Finn were at their desks. Zeus was playing with a scrunched-up piece of paper near them. He saw me and bounded over, his huge kitty paws and gangly legs all kinds of adorable. I shut the door, put my stuff on the table and kneeled. "Hey, little guy. How are you?" He bounced onto my thighs. I scooped him up and snuggled him against me.

Carina got up and came over. She eyed the things on my desk and sniffed. "Ooh, is d'at t'ree delicious-smelling paper bags on your desk?"

I grinned. "Yes. I got three chocolate eclairs—one for each of us. Vinegar's one is to say thank you for looking after Zeus, and yours is because I didn't want to face your wrath if you missed out."

She pointed at me. "You, my lady, are very smart. You never would've heard d'e end of it if I didn't get one." She plucked two off the desk and gave one to Finn on the way back to her workstation.

I gave Zeus one last squeeze and released him. "Wish I could play with you all day, buddy, but I've got a heap to do." I stood, and he pivoted around and chased his paper ball. I sat and got my laptop out, by which time, Zeus had pawed the paper over. He plonked his bottom on the floor and stared up at me.

"He wants you to throw it. We spent half an hour last night playing fetch with his toy penguin."

Carina stared at him with heart eyes. "You love d'at kitty. Admit it. You should be his daddy."

He shook his head. "I can't."

I eyed him for a moment. His face was genuinely sad when he said it. What was really holding him back? Was it that he really didn't want a cat, or was his fear of commitment so bad that it extended to anything alive? "Do you have houseplants?"

His eyebrows dipped down in the middle "A couple. Why?"

I shrugged. "Just wondering how deep your fear of commitment runs."

Carina laughed. "It's deeper d'an d'e Marianas Trench, don't ya know."

He rolled his eyes. "Very funny. Now, if we can kindly drop this discussion, I have work to do."

Carina and I shared a look, and she smirked. He hadn't heard the end of it from either of us. Okay, so it was mean of us to pressure him, but he really was the perfect person—aside from me—to adopt our clever little feline. Zeus pawed my leg. I laughed. "Okay, okay." I picked the paper up and threw it to the back of the room. He zinged after it, batted it around and chased it until he eventually picked it up in his mouth and brought it over. I threw it again… and again… and again. "Okay, buddy. I have to work now. Maybe Auntie Carina will throw it for you?" I threw the paper at her head, but I missed. It landed next to her chair.

She shook her head. "Fine. But just for a couple of minutes."

I took my phone out of my bag to warn Bellamy that I wanted to come down and ask when was a good time, but someone knocked on the office door. Finn looked at me. "I thought you said the first appointment wasn't until one."

"It's not." Hmm, mystery time. No one came to see us here, and Julian wouldn't knock. Okay, so Finn's sister had visited once, but that was it. I stood, went to the door, and opened it.

A skinny guy in his twenties stood there. His beard was down to his chest, and if my eyes didn't deceive me, it had crumbs in it, and what was that stringy green plant matter? I was betting on parsley or maybe rocket. He wore a T-shirt, tracksuit pants with a hole in the knee, and nothing on his dirty feet. Once my brain got on board with that mess, I realised that he wasn't acquainted with deodorant, and maybe not even a shower, and hadn't been for quite some time. I tried not to gag. "Can I help you?"

"I'm here about the cat."

I wasn't sure how he was going to take care of a cat when he clearly couldn't take care of himself, but fair was fair. I'd let him in, and we could spray air freshener later. "Please come in. What's your name?"

"Riley."

"Oh, okay. I thought your appointment was at one today."

He shrugged and picked his nose. I swallowed some vomit. Oh dear lord. "Was it? I don't pay attention to those things. I felt like coming now, so I did."

I stood aside so he could enter. "Would you feed the cat both morning and night? He needs to eat twice a day." Okay, so some cats only ate once a day, but that's what Zeus was used to.

"Maybe. Some days I like to fast. I'm sure the cat can manage. And I'm vegan, so the cat will be too." I had nothing against vegans. In fact, when people did it because they didn't want to eat sentient beings, I had all the respect in the world.

If only I had the willpower, but humans who tried to put their belief systems on helpless animals were another thing. Cats were meat eaters and would eventually starve to death without meat in their diet.

"I'm sorry, but it's not going to work out. Cats eat meat. They can't survive on vegetables alone."

He put his hands on his hips. An extra whiff of stink surrounded me. I coughed. "Says who?"

I gave him a "you have to be kidding me" look. "Nature says. I'm sorry, but I don't think Zeus is a good fit for you, nor is any cat. Dogs can survive without meat. Maybe get one of those or a bird."

No doubt sensing that this guy probably wasn't going to go quietly, Finn and Carina both came to support me, and their faces contorted because of the smell. Finn was way taller than the guy, and he did his best to loom. He pushed his chest out and folded his arms across it. I wasn't swooning. Not. At. All. "Look, mate. I hope we're not going to have any trouble here. If you don't believe Miss Winters, you might want to research on the internet or ask a vet."

The guy scratched his frontal nether regions. Oh, God. Please make it stop. "Fine. Next time, you should put that in the ad. How was I supposed to know?"

My smile was weak as my nostril hairs died. "I'm really sorry. Thanks for coming down, and have a good day."

Finn walked behind him, almost herding him until he was out of the room. Finn followed him out and watched him go down the stairs and through the front door. In the meantime, Carina and I ran to the windows and opened all four of them. I stuck my head out and breathed the fresh air, as did she. We looked across at each other as we tasted the sweet outside air. I started laughing. Which started her laughing. But then Zeus noticed the windows were open, and he jumped up onto the ledge next to me. "Yikes!" I grabbed him. I had no idea if kittens had height awareness—kind of like how little kids had no road sense. "We're going to have to shut the windows," I called to her on the outside.

"Let me have a couple more breat's, lovie."

"Okay." I leaned back in, bringing Zeus with me, and closed the window. "Sorry to spoil your fun, kitty, but that's definitely not safe."

Finn had shut the door and then the window above his desk while Carina took care of her window and the one between them. Finn shook his head. "How can it be so ridiculously difficult to find someone to adopt one cat?"

"I don't know." Now I had a sense of what Rosa had experienced. I'd written her off as a bad cat mother who was passing the buck, but maybe she'd tried, and it was almost impossible to find someone suitable. I couldn't blame her for handing him to me. I was probably the first not-too-crazy person to meet Zeus, and I was capable of keeping him alive and safe, and even giving him a cuddle. I had to hand one thing to her—she was a good judge of character. It was just a shame that I had a crabby landlady. Who might be understandably crabby. Which reminded me.

I went back to my desk and called Bellamy. "Hello, Sergeant."

"Hello, Miss Winters. Have you decided to take Miss Stick's case on?"

"Um, possibly, but this is about something else. Also, don't tell her I'm helping yet. I want her to stew a bit." Wow, I was being super honest right now. Oh well. If he ended up having a lower opinion of me, I'd survive. Besides, I was used to people in my life being disappointed in me. Who knew it would be a good skill?

"That's not very nice. I know she's given you a hard time

but—"

"No, Sergeant, it's not very nice. But maybe this will teach her a lesson. I actually doubt it, but it's worth trying." *And it also makes me feel like I'm not such a pushover. At least give me that.*

"It's your call, but I won't lie—I'm a bit disappointed."

I smiled. "I hate to disappoint you, but I'll live with it. It won't be the first time someone's been disappointed in me. So, about what I was calling about…."

"Yes. What is it?"

"I need to bring a locket in. I found it when I was walking yesterday, and I think it could be linked to an older, unsolved disappearance." I couldn't say murder because my colleagues were within hearing distance.

He was silent for a moment. "Do you know that because you've spoken to a ghost?"

"Yes."

"Did the ghost tell you where to find the locket?"

"No. It was a coincidence, but anyway, I'd rather not talk about it over the phone. Can I come and see you now?" Carina and Finn had gone back to work, but they were both shooting glances my way. At least I could explain this away because of the link with Mrs Crabby and her daughter going missing.

"Fine, come in, but I don't know how much help I can give you right now. We've been busy with the usual stuff—alcohol-related violence, theft, assault, et cetera, et cetera, and Miss Stick's parents are on my case. Honestly, some days I wish I was in London where the locals wouldn't think of harassing the police. This part of the world is altogether too small." He huffed at the end. I heard someone excuse themselves and say his name.

"That's fine. I'll see you soon. Bye, Sergeant."

"Bye."

I stood, and this time my friends were openly staring. Finn was the first to ask, "What locket, and what disappearance?"

"I found a locket and chain on my walk yesterday, at the edge of the forest. I put it in the paper, thinking it was just something someone would be missing, but Mrs Crabby called about it. It was her daughter's." They looked at me as if to say "so?" "Her daughter went missing over thirty years ago when she was a teenager. She's presumed murdered."

Finn gave me a look that said he wanted to know more, and Carina's eyes widened. "Ooh, lovie, you're always finding d'e good stuff. Do you have a radar or somet'ing?"

I held my hands up in an "I don't know" gesture. "Since I've been hit by lightning, I seem to be in the vicinity of dead bodies a lot. This may or may not be part of it. Or England has a load more murders than Australia has, and I'm cursed to be in the wrong place at the wrong time?" At this point, a curse would be more believable to Finn than me saying I could talk to ghosts. "Anyway, I'm taking it to Bellamy now, and after that, I have some research for an article." I didn't want to tell them I was working on Joyless's case, and I was going to hit up that pool hall. It would be weird to grab a drink or bite to eat there by myself, but if I had a chance to talk to that ghost, I was going to take it, and there was no way I could explain it to any of my friends, so solo it was.

I put my stuff in my bag and gave Zeus a cuddle. "I'll be back before the next interview."

"What time is it?" asked Finn.

"Two, that's if the person respects the time I gave them." I rolled my eyes.

Carina laughed and looked at Finn. "I still say you should take him, Finny. Your excuses have been flimsy at best."

He pressed his lips together and shook his head. Without saying anything, he turned to his screen and went back to work. Someone wasn't happy. Carina and I shared an "ooh, now, we've pushed him too far" look; then I mouthed, "Good luck," and left.

I hurried home to get Daisy, then drove to Cramptonbury. My phone, which was in a holder on the dash, dinged with a message. Meg's name flashed on the screen. As soon as I parked outside the station, I read the message. *Haven't seen you for ages. Can we catch up for dinner tonight at your place? I'll bring the food.*

My initial reaction was to ask why it was at my place, but maybe something had happened, and she didn't want to talk about it in front of people. *Of course. How's six thirty? Also, I can cook if you like.*

No! Dad made a huge lasagne last night, and we have heaps. I'm bringing garlic bread too. If you could just open a bottle of red, it would be much appreciated. 😉 🍷

I can do that 😆. *Is everything okay?*

Kind of. I'll talk to you tonight. Later xx.

Okay, later xx. My mouth turned down in a sad pout. Now I was going to worry about her until I knew what was wrong. Argh. Surely if it was super bad, she would've called me. On a scale of one to ten, this might be a five or six, maybe a seven. If it was higher, she would've told me in person, and she probably wouldn't be hungry for lasagne and garlic bread. Okay, now that I'd talked myself into the fact that Meg's problem would keep until tonight, I grabbed my bag and got out of the car.

PC Davis was at the front desk today. The redheaded constable smiled. "Morning, Miss Winters. How's the crime-solving going?"

I grinned. At least he wasn't offended by my side gig. "Good… I think. I have something for Sergeant Bellamy to chase up, actually. Something that needs a real police person to deal with. My research and hunches can only get me so far."

"They seem to get you pretty far." He pressed the button to release the security door. "Go on in."

"Thanks, Constable." I strode through the familiar hallway, marvelling at how many times I'd done it, and now it was almost part of a normal day. In the early days, I was so nervous when I came here, and to be fair, Bellamy wasn't exactly welcoming. I'd slowly worn him down, and now he was the only one here who knew my secret. I would never have believed it would play out like this if you'd told me when I first arrived in Manesbury. Funny how life worked out sometimes.

His door was open, and he saw me walking through the main office area. "Come in, Miss Winters. Shut the door after yourself."

I did as asked. Sergeant Fox and Charles weren't here for a change, not that it mattered. I reached into my bag, brought out the locket, and put it on Bellamy's desk. "I found this yesterday morning. I'm sorry to say that I washed it. It was caked in mud, and it was hard to tell any details, and I wanted to put a picture of it in the paper."

"This picture?" He turned his monitor around and showed me my article.

"That's the one."

He picked up the jewellery and inspected it, inside and out. "And who do you think it belongs to?"

"Everly Collins, Margaret Collins's daughter. Her ghost lives with me in my flat. It used to be hers. When she first appeared in front of me, she had a nasty slash across her throat, which would've been fatal. She said she doesn't know where her body is. Apparently her date killed her." Bellamy's mouth dropped open. I wasn't sure if it was because I was talking so casually about a conversation I'd had with a ghost or if it was because I could so easily solve a decades-old murder. "Anyway, Mrs Collins called the paper and asked about the locket, saying it was her daughter's, which is how I discovered that Everly is her daughter. Everly wasn't forthcoming about that, which is unfortunate because I've complained to her about her mother several times."

He raised a brow, one corner of his mouth following. "Only you could put your foot in it with a ghost, Miss Winters."

"Yes, well, I'm one of kind. Anyway, Everly doesn't like talking about her murder, so I'm not sure how helpful she'll be if I have any other questions."

"I'm sure it's traumatic for her." He slid his keyboard over and looked to his right, at the monitor he'd slid off to the side so he could talk to me. He typed for a bit. "Ah, here's the file. That's an old case. I'm going to have to ask for the archived files to be brought in. They'd be in storage somewhere." He slid the computer back again and stared at the locket. "Can you show me where exactly you found it?"

"Yep. Do you have time this arvo or tomorrow?"

"Tomorrow would probably be better. I'll call you."

"Okay, thanks."

He changed the subject without warning. "Any news about Miss Stick's case?"

"Yes, actually. Charles found the ghost I was looking for. His underworld name is Ironfist McTavish, real name Donald Arthur McTavish. He was criminally active in maybe the 1920s to 1950s. His ghost looks like he died in maybe his sixties, but I'm not sure. If he drank a lot and smoked, he might look older than he is."

"Interesting. Do you mind if I look him up?"

I shrugged. "Be my guest. I don't take it as an insult. The more you can prove what I'm saying, the saner I look." I grinned. It was a goal of mine to appear to be sane. It wasn't nearly as easy as it sounded.

He chuckled. "Indeed." He punched away at his keyboard, and I sat back and waited, which gave me thinking time. I didn't know why Everly refused to tell me who killed her. Did she still love him? Surely not. I sat up straight, my heart beating quickly. What I was about to suggest was going to upset her, no doubt, but I had to. "Sergeant?"

He didn't take his eyes off what he was doing. "Yes?"

"I know how I can find out who killed Everly, and then we'll just need to prove it."

That stopped him typing. He peered at me. "How?"

"Maybe her mother would know who killed her. To be honest, there would've been a lot of blood at the time, and I have no idea how the murderer got away with it."

His fingers drummed the tabletop. "I don't know, Miss Winters. Do we want to open that wound with Mrs Collins when we have nothing else to go on except this locket? Besides, the police would've looked into everyone who knew Everly at the time. I doubt Mrs Collins has any new information that's going to help."

I sighed. "I guess you're right." The only one who could help me was Everly, and she didn't want to. "Maybe I can get Everly to talk to me about it. If she's been trying to protect her mother's sanity, she won't want me bringing it up with her. It's a low thing to do, but I could tell her I'm going to speak to her mum about it if she doesn't tell me what happened."

He sat back, his gaze intensifying. "Miss Winters, that's cruel. I can't condone that."

"Even if it will bring Mrs Collins closure and solve a murder? What if the murderer is still out there? What if they've killed others?"

"I must say, this is... unusual. Taking the deceased's feelings into account isn't covered in our procedure manual." He slumped back against his chair and massaged his temples. I didn't want to traumatise Everly any more than she already had been, so I'd give him time to come up with something, anything that might help. He finally looked at me. "Based on what you've said, I doubt she'd want to come here, but maybe I could visit you and communicate via you." He sat up straighter. "I'm going to do some more digging, see if any similar murders or missing persons' cases have come up since Everly was killed. If her killer has murdered others, it might sway her decision to out the person. What kind of a woman is she?"

"She's caring, nice, friendly. She works with other ghosts and helps them through their problems. She wanted to be a psychologist before she died."

He stared at me and blinked. I couldn't help smiling. This was a lot for him to deal with—us speaking of the dead and their "lives" like it was normal. "Right. Okay." He cleared his throat. "I'm going to keep digging into Ironfist and Everly's murder, and I'll let you know when I have something. Okay?"

"Sounds fine to me. As long as we're working towards answers, I'm happy." I stood. "Thanks, Sergeant. I know this is… a lot. I appreciate you believing me about everything."

He smiled. "I'm surprising myself, to be honest." He chuckled. "Anyway, I've got a lot to do. Just let me know when you've got any more information."

"Will do. Have a good afternoon."

"You too, Miss Winters." By the time I shut his door, he was already focussed on his screen. Hopefully those files on Everly's disappearance hadn't vanished like her body. Unfortunately, I knew getting those files from storage could take a while. Poor Mrs Crabby had been waiting over thirty years for an answer. I supposed she could wait a few more weeks.

The Stick and Balls Sports Bar was located on a main road on the edge of a large village. When I'd imagined it during my conversation with Charles, I'd thought of a dingy, dirty, smoke-filled bar with billiards tables and maybe a dartboard, the customers barely functioning alcoholics. I was partly wrong. It wasn't smoke-filled, and the patrons were sober… at least most of them, although it was early in the day.

I went to the bar and ordered an orange juice. The bartender, a middle-aged gent with a handlebar moustache, was pleasant enough. I thanked him and chose a ripped orange barstool towards the end of the bar, close to the billiard tables. There was only one table being played, and a group of three ghosts stood around it. When the young guy making a shot missed getting the red ball into the pouch, the ghosts laughed and heckled him.

So, this was what my quarry did for fun when he wasn't confirming murder plots were successful.

I took another hit of the orange juice and wondered how I was going to talk to the crim. I'd have to use the old "talking to someone on the phone" trick, but it wasn't as if I could stand near the ghosts without someone wondering why I was so close to their snooker game. Hmm, the dartboards were near there.

I took my drink and placed it on a high table that sat a few feet from the ghosts and was close to where I'd stand to throw darts. I collected the darts from a cupboard that sat under three evenly spaced dartboards that were attached to black-boards where, I assumed, people wrote their scores. I had practically no experience, having played about twice in my life.

This was going to be embarrassing. The things I did to uncover the truth.

The two guys playing snooker gave me a once-over. I

scowled and turned my back to them, wanting to make sure they knew I didn't want to talk to them. Once I'd engaged my "do not approach" vibe, I stood behind the line on the floor, took aim, ignored the nerves taunting me that I'd miss the board entirely, and drew in a lungful of air. Something I'd learned from my years of playing sport was that your body performed better when your breathing was right. I threw on my exhale.

Ooh, that wasn't too bad. For a start, I'd managed to land it on the board—yay me—and secondly, it landed next to the section I'd been aiming for. Instead of getting twenty points, I ended up with five, but it was in the section near the bull's-eye. I readied my next dart.

"That wench got lucky, and look at those peachy cheeks. I'd love to get my hands on those."

My eyebrows rose, and fury pulsed in my veins. I spun around. The guys playing pool weren't even watching me, but the three ghosts were. It had been one of them, and they obviously thought I'd never hear them. Ironfist stopped laughing when he recognised me, but a dangerous edge sharpened his smile. "I know you."

I slid my phone out of my pocket and pretended to answer it while I made eye contact with the ghost for a moment. "Oh, hey, Donald, I heard some rumours that you were a total loser." I turned away so I wasn't facing the snooker players or the ghosts and spoke just loud enough for the ghosts to hear me. I held up one hand and wiggled my pinky finger. "And a dud in bed." If the non-ghosts heard me, they'd peg me as the biggest cow on earth. Also, I hoped my insults were enough to goad the ghost into coming over where I could speak more quietly and face to face. I wanted to see his expression. It was always easier to get information if you had body language to go with the words.

Yes! It worked. Donald Ironfist McTavish appeared in front of me, his huge belly almost touching mine. I resisted the urge to step away. Showing weakness would give him back control, and if that happened, I could wave bye-bye to any information.

He was no longer smiling.

"What did you say, trollop?"

I chuckled. Trollop might have been an insult when he was alive, but that was zero to mild on today's charts. "I said that you have a small…." I gestured to his nether regions.

He tried to choke me with both hands. I felt a chill… and slight pressure. I kept the shock from my face because it would never be enough to hurt me. "I'll kill you!"

"Hard to do when you're impotent." I was really talking about the fact that, as a ghost, he couldn't do anything to me, but the double entendre didn't hurt… well, maybe it hurt him. I ignored the fact that he was a poltergeist—a weak one, but one nonetheless.

"I was one of the best hitmen of my time. Who are you to insult me? Useless woman. I wouldn't even take the time to spit in your face."

"If you could." I winked and grinned.

He pulled out a ghost gun and pulled the trigger. Nothing happened. His face screwed up in disgust, and he threw the weapon at my head. I managed to hold it together enough not to duck, and it flew straight through me.

"Oh no, poor little boy's having a tantrum. I'm surprised someone trusted your competence enough to help them murder Alan."

"Mr Chandler knows I'm the best. I was when I was alive, and I am now."

"Hmm, maybe Mr Chandler couldn't afford anyone better." That was a stupid statement since you couldn't give a ghost money, but the more info I squeezed out of him, the better. "Anyway, you can't so much as touch someone in this world. You're no better than an errand boy."

He narrowed his eyes and tried to poke me in the chest with a finger. I ignored the icy stabs that had enough force to indent my skin and suppressed the urge to push him away. *Show no fear.* "He has more money than you could spend in a lifetime, and he trusted me to make sure Alan the scumbag was dead. I did my bit." He bared yellowed teeth. "He would've got me to do all of it if I was alive." He slammed his fist into his palm. "Instead, he got some other fancy hitman—"

"Hey, Ironfist, stop playing with the tramp. We're gettin' out of 'ere." Oh no. Why did he have to interrupt when it was going so well? I'd just proven—to myself at least—that Joyless wasn't responsible.

I narrowed my eyes. "So, Joy didn't do it. But why did he frame her?" Now I had to feel bad about her. Damn it. There was no way I could let her rot in jail now. Boy, did I feel sorry for myself.

One side of his top lip arrowed up in a not-quite smile and a not-quite sneer. "Why not?"

"Come on, mate. Let's go." His comrade—a skinny, middle-aged guy with a horde of tattoos crowding his arms, joined us. He gave me a once-over, which I ignored.

Ironfist gave him a nod and turned to me, a murderous haze in his eyes. "You give my boss any trouble, and we'll see who's laughing then, Avery Winters." With that, he disappeared.

How did he know my name?

You know the feeling you get half an hour after you've left home when you realise you've left the iron on, face down on the ironing board? I had it, and it sucked.

CHAPTER 8

I made it back to the office just before lunchtime. When I checked my emails, the person who was coming to see about Zeus this afternoon had cancelled. "Nooooo! Why?"

Carina was out, but Finn looked over at me. "What's wrong?" I told him. His face fell. "Oh. And that's it? No one else wants to have a look?"

"No." I put my elbows on the table and sunk my head into my hands. What was I going to do? As much as I teased Finn about having the cat, he really didn't want the responsibility, and forcing Zeus on someone wasn't right. What else could I do? I raised my head and looked at Finn. "Do you think you could mind him for just one more night?"

"Is one more night going to turn into three more, ten more, a hundred more?"

My chest tightened as I looked across at the sweetheart sleeping next to Finn's laptop. I couldn't let Zeus down. "No. I promise. I'm going to start looking at new places to rent. I should be able to find something that allows pets, and then I can take him." Saying the words out loud, they felt true—I did want Zeus. Unfortunately, the fear of not being able to find something else was scary. "There is the little matter of me being in a lease, but maybe if I annoy Mrs Crabby enough, she'll kick me out." The irony of fearing being kicked out for so long, and now I wanted it to happen.

"I'd hold off on getting kicked out until you find something else. The rental market is pretty tight."

"Yeah, thanks for the reality check because I have so many other options right now." I narrowed my eyes and gave him my crankiest cranky face. "That's the best I can come up with. If you're going to be such a buzzkill, can you at least give me an alternative?" Maybe I was coming across a bit snarky, but that's because I was. I couldn't be all sunshine and chocolate cake all the time.

He stroked Zeus's back. "Fine. I'll take him for a couple more nights, until you know what you're doing. Maybe Josie could take him for a while?"

I sat up straighter. Why hadn't I thought of that? Our neighbour across the way was a lovely woman, and she already had a cat, so she shouldn't be allergic. I was sure she'd be only too happy to help. "Oh, that's not a bad idea. I'll ask her when I go home. Thanks."

His "Don't mention it" was laced with annoyance. "You and C don't appreciate me enough. I'm awesome, dammit!"

A small laugh escaped. "Oh, thank God. I thought you were being serious for a moment."

He gave a wry smile. "I half was. I know you want the best for the cat, but I'm honestly not the answer. There's lots of travelling in my future. I want to spend time in Europe, then I'm thinking of South America. Obviously I have to save up for a few years first, but cats live a long time. I don't want to bond with one and then leave it a few years into its life."

Oh, wow, that information shouldn't have hurt as much as it did. Not that I thought I was going to be here forever, but how much time did I have left with him? I kept my voice light, as if one day never seeing him again didn't bother me in the slightest. "Right, of course. Why didn't you just say so before?"

He shrugged one shoulder. "It's a fair way off, and I didn't want the terrible two convincing me that my travel plans weren't as important as the cat."

"Ha, we're the terrible two. I love it."

He shook his head and rolled his eyes. "Okay, well, now that's sorted, I have to get back to work."

It was depressing that I liked him enough to know I was going to miss him one day, and that day was going to come sooner than I'd considered. Why was I even thinking about this? He was a friend—one I clearly had a crush on—but he would never be more than that, and it was okay for me to miss him… just not too much.

Get your head out of the fog, Avery. Besides, my life was pretty darn good now… so much better than I'd ever had and that I'd honestly believed it could be. It was greedy to want too much. Being happy with my now was important, and I would be. No more thinking about the hottie sitting on the other side of the room.

It was time to work and try and find out who this rich Mr Chandler was. Which reminded me—I should call Bellamy and tell him what I'd found out. Maybe he could help uncover who this guy was… the guy who was behind Alan's murder.

❧

On my way home, I stopped in to see Josie. She was only too happy to look after Zeus, but she couldn't keep him because she already had a cat—a cat who didn't like other animals.

She'd keep Zeus in his own room, and she said she'd be fine with looking after him for a two to three weeks. I thanked her profusely and continued on my way home.

I stopped outside the front gate and stared at the door. How was I going to deal with Mrs Crabby now I was aware of her secret? If only I knew if she was just horrible because she was born that way or if she'd become so from grief. There was no way I could be mean to her knowing everything she'd been through. First Joy, and now this. I must've done something to tick someone off in a previous life. I thought I'd had enough bad juju to last a lifetime. Apparently I was wrong.

With my shiny new attitude towards Mrs Crabby—I wasn't giving up the name because it was all I had left—I sucked in a huge breath and went up the pathway. I unlocked the door quietly, not because I didn't want to get into trouble, but because I wanted to be extra considerate. Okay, it would also be nice not to get into trouble.

I made it halfway up the stairs before I looked back. Nope, still no sign of her. Was that why she hadn't come out last night or this morning? Had the locket thrown her into a fresh wave of grief? It must've come as a shock. She was probably reliving the nightmare all over again, and still she didn't know what happened to her daughter.

I let myself into my flat. Everly sat on the couch, picking at her top. "Hey, Avery."

"Hey. Are you feeling any better?"

She shook her head. "Not really."

I put my stuff on the dining table and went and sat next to her. "I know your secret."

Her bewildered expression made her look about five years younger than she was. "Mrs Collins called about the locket today." The least I could do was not call her Mrs Crabby in front of Everly any more.

Her eyes glistened, and her lip trembled. Her voice was a whisper. "You know?"

I tried to pat her hand, but mine went straight through. We both stared at her hand as I said, "Yes. She called about the locket. She knows it's been found, but I've given it to Sergeant Bellamy. She'll get it back when they're done with it."

She sniffled. Her chin fell to her chest.

"Why didn't you want me to know she was your mum? She didn't have anything to do with your disappearance, did she?" It hadn't occurred to me before, and I still didn't think that was the case, but it made sense, so I had to make sure.

Her head snapped up, her eyes wide with indignation. "Of course not! She's my mother. She loves me."

"Sorry. I had to ask. I just can't understand why you wouldn't want the person caught. Your mum needs closure."

She shook her head, her eyes begging me for I didn't know what. "You don't understand. She'd never forgive herself."

"What? Why?"

She leapt to her feet. "I can't, okay. I just can't. I'm sorry." A tear tracked down her cheek. Before I could ask her to change her mind, she disappeared.

I slumped back and stared at the ceiling. Whyyyyyyyyy? My heavy sigh deflated my chest. This didn't make sense. If she didn't want to stir things up again, it was too late. If her mother didn't have anything to do with it, why would she never forgive herself? Surely she didn't mean for letting her go out when she did. She was at an age that she wouldn't have even asked for her permission.

I pondered the problem as I vacuumed, then showered. By the time Meg buzzed from downstairs, I was no closer to an answer. I let her in and pushed the problem to the back of my brain—it wasn't like I could discuss it with Meg, except in a super roundabout way, and from her message, she had enough on her plate.

She knocked. I opened the door and gave her a huge hug, which she reciprocated with one arm because her other was holding a canvas bag full of food.

"Hey, gorgeous. Come in."

I observed her as she entered. She looked the same as always, and her eyes weren't red from crying. Hopefully whatever had happened was only a three or four on a scale of one to ten.

Meg put the bag of food on the table and slung her purse on a chair. I took the food containers out of the bag. "This smells del—" I jerked my head to look at her. Yep, that was a sob I'd heard. "Oh my God. What's wrong?" This apartment had seen its share of tears today.

"It's Chris. He… he broke up with me."

I gasped and threw my arms around my weeping friend. "I'm so sorry. What stupid excuse did he give?" Maybe I sounded harsh, but I always had my friends' backs, and part of that was getting angry on their behalf.

"He said our relationship's run its course, and that he thought he could do the long-distance thing, but he can't." Her body shook, and I squeezed her tighter.

"It's going to be okay. I promise. Why don't we sit on the couch." I led her to said couch and sat her down. "I'll get you a tissue and a glass of red. How does that sound?" She took a shuddering breath and nodded. I grabbed everything quickly, including a glass of wine for myself, and returned to the couch. "Here you go."

She took the tissue and glass. "Thank you. I'm sorry for just unloading like that." She blew her nose. "It happened yesterday, and I thought… I thought I was handling it. Apparently I wasn't." Her smile was small, but at least it was there.

"What did Bails say?"

She pouted. "He's been busy with his girlfriend, and I didn't want to tell him while we were working in case this happened." She gestured to her face.

"Fair enough. Gee, he's really ramped up his relationship with Stella. At least she's nice." She was also supermodel gorgeous. I'd definitely missed the boat there, but funnily enough, that didn't bother me as much as the thought of Finn leaving Manesbury and flying off into the sunset. Interesting. *Not.*

"Yeah, she's nice. I would've preferred he date you, but if he's going to date someone else, it might as well be Stella." Her gaze raked my face. "Do you regret not seeing where things might have gone? He really liked you, you know."

He was gorgeous and sweet, and I did regret it a little bit, but not enough. "Yes and no. He's a great guy, and I do think he's attractive, but I wasn't ready, and I'm still not. Besides, if anything bad happened between us, it would've been mega awkward. I'd rather not risk our friendship."

"Fair enough. I won't bug you about it again, but I still think you guys could've been great."

"Probably, but we'll never know." I had a sip of wine. "Now, tell me, do we want to put out a hit on Chris or what?"

CHAPTER 9

The next morning, my first port of call was the police station and Sergeant Bellamy, but on my way down the stairs at home, I made sure to be noisy. I was testing out my theory that Mrs Crabby wasn't herself. I slammed my apartment door and stomped down the stairs. I opened the front door without her intervention. Something was very wrong. I couldn't let this go, so I did the stupidest thing ever for someone who was happy to avoid her, and I knocked on her door.

It took a minute, but she answered it. Still in her purple dressing gown, she had under-eye bags that matched. "What do you want?"

I gave her a sad smile. "Hi, Mrs Collins. Your words are yours, but the energy you delivered them with is a bit off... maybe too mild."

She stared at me, speechless for a moment. That was a first. "Your point being?"

This wasn't easy to bring up, and my palms were sweaty, but I couldn't let her go through this alone. I wanted her to know that even if she didn't want to share, she had the option. "I'm the one who found the locket, and I know the history. I'm sorry this has brought everything up for you again about Everly." She winced. "I want you to know that if you need anything, even if it's someone to have a cup of tea with and chat, I'm here. And before you get cranky with me and slam the door in my face, I know we're not exactly friends, but I do care whether or not you're okay." If not for any other fact than she was Everly's mother, and she'd experienced something horrific. We had our differences, but my heart wasn't totally shrivelled up… yet.

Grief shadowed her face, then surprise. "Right, okay." She looked over my shoulder before meeting my eyes. "Thank you, Avery. I won't take you up on your offer, but your concern is noted." She stepped back and shut the door. At least she hadn't slammed it.

I drove to the station knowing I'd done the right thing, but it might not be enough. I'd consider what else I should do for Mrs Crabby later. Maybe Everly would be composed enough tonight to talk about it and let me know how I could help her mother.

PC Adams buzzed me through the security door. The whole gang was waiting in Bellamy's office. I shut the door before I said, "Hello, everyone."

Fox and Charles said hello at the same time as Bellamy. Bellamy shook his head. "Are you telling me your friends are here again?"

"Yep. Sergeant Fox and Charles."

"It's disconcerting thinking ghosts are watching me work, and I have no clue." He looked around the room, trying to see the unseeable.

"If there was some way for me to help you see them, I'd do it. Truth be told, that would help me a lot, too—I could prove to people that I wasn't a loon. As you know, if Vinegar ever got wind of this, he'd never speak to me again."

"Well, I'm never going to tell him, so you have nothing to worry about."

"And when Joy tells him, will you stick up for me?" She didn't make idle threats. It made me not want to help her, but having her owe me one was probably a good thing. Another point for me telling her I'd help, even if she lost respect for me… not that she had any in the first place. Hmm, it was just my own self-respect I was worried about.

He folded his arms and leaned back. "Why would you think she'd do that?"

"Because she told me she would if I didn't help her."

"But you're helping her, aren't you?"

I laced my hands together in my lap. "Yes, but if she does get out, the next time I do something she doesn't like, I'll bet my rental that she threatens me with it. Who knows? She might even tell him just for fun." She really was an inferior human.

"Of course I'll stand up for you if that happens, but let's not jump the gun. I find it's easier to deal with reality than supposition. Which brings me to my next question. What information do you have for me regarding the case?"

"I went to the snooker hall yesterday, and the ghost was there. I managed to get him to talk a bit. He let slip that his boss, who isn't Joy, arranged for Alan to be murdered. The boss's surname is Chandler. I don't know what he does, where he lives, or his first name. He apparently has a lot of money, though. I know it's not much, but it's a start. He used a hitman to help do it."

"I don't suppose you have any information on who that might be."

I gave him an apologetic shake of my head. "Unfortunately not. I figured we needed to work backwards from Alan. See if anything led from him to a Mr Chandler."

He picked up a blue file that was sitting near his right arm and pulled out a pile of paper, then leafed through them. He paid particular attention to a list on one of the pages. "Nope. No mention here of any Mr Chandler as a friend, boss, enemy, or family."

"Have you gone through his phone?" I hoped my question wasn't insulting. It was more that I wanted an answer for myself than me thinking they hadn't done that yet.

His tone told me that I'd managed to offend him. "Of course, Miss Winters. That's one of the first things we did. There was no Mr Chandler in the phone, and we contacted everyone on his contacts list."

"I could try and contact Alan. I don't know if he's passed all the way over, but if I could go to his house and call for him, if he's around, he'll likely come. That's providing he doesn't live with anyone because I'd look rather loopy." I could've suggested the coffee shop, but there was no way I could be there alone, and he might be avoiding his place of death, depending on how upset he was.

"I'm afraid that might be difficult. He did live by himself in a house, but I think his sister has moved in to pack up all his things. They're going to rent it out until the will has been sorted." He drummed his fingers on the table. "We could tell her we need to look through his bedroom one more time, and I'll attend and keep her out of your way if need be."

I smiled. "Thank you. If he's still around, that's going to be much easier than trying to figure out who this Mr Chandler is. I had a quick Google last night, and there are thousands of people this side of London with that surname. We could rule out some of them quickly, of course, but we'd still be left with too many to interview. It would be an impossible task."

Amusement brightened his face. "Yes, impossible, especially with our staffing levels." His gaze flicked to the computer monitor before coming back to me. "I've ordered the files on Miss Collins's disappearance. They probably won't be here for at least two weeks, maybe four. They couldn't give me a firm timeline."

I tapped both feet on the floor. That was such a long time. Compared to how long ago Everly went missing, it wasn't, but in my life, it was. I wanted to solve this ASAP and give Mrs Collins closure. If only I could figure out why Everly was against it. If I managed that, I could come up with a plan of attack to break down her hesitation. "It is what it is, I suppose." I held up my hand. "Can we put this conversation on hold for a sec? I want to ask Charles something."

"Of course." He peered at me with interest as I turned to the ghost sitting next to me.

"Do you know why Everly won't talk about her murder?" They were pretty close. If anyone knew the answer, it would be Charles.

He swung his legs back and forth. "Nope. She never talks about it. I asked once, and she got annoyed with me, so I never mentioned it again."

I sighed. "Okay, thanks. Do you have anything to add that might help either of these cases?"

He looked at Fox. Fox shook his head. Charles shrugged. "Nope. The sergeant and I will see if we can find out anything else about Mr Chandler if you like, but I don't know how successful we'll be. I can't follow Ironfist anywhere—I have to rely on our informants."

I chuckled. "You have informants?"

Fox cleared his throat. "What else would you call them, Miss Winters? They help law enforcement and keep an eye out. I've had a network for years. If Ironfist shows up anywhere my eyes and ears are, we'll know about it. I have them looking out. It's the best I can do."

"I appreciate it, Sergeant."

Sergeant Bellamy leaned to the side to meet my gaze. "Are you talking to me or…?"

I laughed. "Or. Sergeant Fox is in his usual spot next to your chair. Sometimes he stands behind it."

Bellamy shuddered. "Please don't tell me that."

"You have nothing to worry about. Sergeant Fox is a kind person and an upstanding policeman. He's not going to go all poltergeist on you."

Bellamy's eyes shot wide. "You mean poltergeists exist?"

"Yes, and some of them are—for want of a better word— evil. They can move things. Charles has been trying to work up to that, so if you see anything moving in your office that shouldn't be, let me know. He hasn't cracked it yet, but if he does, he'll be a huge help to us; I'm sure." I was originally hoping to use Charles to ferret through Bellamy's papers when he wasn't letting me in on a case, but now that was redun-dant… at least this week. I held in my chuckle. Things changed quickly around here, so who knew when I'd need Charles's help to grab info from the police. The way Bellamy changed his mind was worse than me when the waiter was standing there, and I couldn't decide between chocolate cake and a lemon tart.

He put his hand up. "I don't want to know any more. If you can give me a moment, I'll make a call and see when we can get in. Do you have any preferences for a day and time?"

"I've got an interview at two today, so any time before twelve or after three. Failing that, tomorrow is open all day so far." I wanted to pop in and check on Meg before my two o'clock. She'd been so-so when she'd left last night, and she needed some extra love and care until she'd been through the worst of the post-breakup blues. Seemed like there was a lot of negative energy flying around at the moment.

He gave a nod, picked up his landline phone, found the number he was looking for, and dialled. His conversation—on speaker—was short and, thankfully, sweet. Alan's sister had no problem with us going now. She was heading out but would leave the spare key in a pot plant and we were to leave it on the kitchen bench.

We stood. Bellamy strapped his duty belt on, and I hefted my handbag over my shoulder. I gave Charles and Fox a wave. "See you guys later."

Bellamy stopped and stared at me. He shook his head and headed for the door. "Come on. You can follow me in your car."

Alan's house was midway between Cramptonbury and Manesbury, halfway up a hill. It was separated from the street by a waist-high stone fence. I drove my car between the stone pillars and parked in front of the double garage, next to Bellamy. I got out and locked Daisy.

The house was more impressive than I was expecting for an unengaged or unmarried young man. It was a sprawling rendered bungalow. Large, round white pots full of dormant lavender sat on either side of the three stairs up to the front verandah, the silvery green foliage pretty against the all-white domicile. I walked up the steps and waited for Bellamy to grab the key from one of the pots and unlock the door.

Alan had some style. The designer blue-and-white tiles on the front porch looked like something you'd see in a magazine. My gaze moved to Bellamy, who was wrestling with the keys. "Worst part of my job." He slid the key he'd been jiggling around out of the lock and stuck in the next one. He swore and jerked his fingers back, leaving the key in the lock. He waved his hand around as his face twisted in pain.

"Do you want me to try?" I'd been there before—a red, sore index finger, mangled from a stubborn lock.

"No! I'll get it." He'd made it a personal vendetta. Bellamy wasn't a quitter. I held in my giggle as he grunted with the effort of trying to tame the door. Hopefully the third key would be the charm… since it was the last one left. He tried it, and it turned with ease. He pushed the door open, and I followed him in. I shut it and walked down the wide entry hallway until it came to another hallway to our left and a large opening straight in front of us through which I could see two living areas stacked one after the other, the view clear to the back of the house where picture windows looked over an amazing rural view.

"Nice."

"Yes. He had a fair bit of money for a young fellow." Bellamy's serious police face gave nothing away.

"Anything suspicious?"

"Not that we could find." He started off down the other corridor.

"Actually, since his sister isn't here, I can just try now."

He stopped walking. "Are you sure?"

"Yep." I imagined Alan as he was at the coffee shop, alive and pushing Joyless's buttons.

"Why are you smiling, Miss Winters?"

"Um… no reason." I cleared my throat and straightened my face. "Alan, if you're still around, please come and speak to me at your house. It's Avery from the coffee shop on the day you died. The one who could see you. Alan?"

Bellamy stared at the space between us. "Is he here yet?"

"No. I'll tell you if he appears." I turned around and raised my voice a bit. "Alan?"

He faded in, wearing the same clothes as the day he died. He'd regained his colour, which was good. I didn't much want to look at someone with blue lips.

"Yes!" I turned to Bellamy. "He's here." He gave a nod. I turned back to Alan. "Hey, do you remember me?"

"Yes, the woman from the coffee shop. You also said it when you called me. So, why did you call me, and who's that?"

"That's Sergeant Bellamy. He's investigating your case, and he got me access to the house while your sister is out. I can't exactly have these"—I motioned to him, then me—"conversations in polite company."

He gave a dry smile. "Understandable. And why do you want to talk to me?"

I found it interesting that he didn't ask about how the case was going, unless he knew because he'd seen his sister talk about it? "I want to know who Mr Chandler is."

My years of journalistic experience told me that the lines on his forehead were legit. "I don't know. I've never heard of him before. Did he help Joy kill me?"

I hated to be the one to admit it, but… "No. We don't think Joy did kill you."

His jaw bunched. "What do you mean, you don't think she killed me? She handed me the goddamned coffee! Of course she killed me." Anger radiated off him. I couldn't blame him.

"She did, yes, but we think she was set up because it was easy to access the café and tamper with things. Whoever did this knew you went in there occasionally."

"How would they know I was going to be there that morning at that time, hmm?"

Good question. "I don't know, but we're working on it. We have evidence that might prove that she's innocent." The look he shot my way said he didn't believe she was innocent for a second. "Look, if you can just put your disbelief aside for a few minutes, I need to ask you some questions."

"Fine, but let it go on record that I think she did it."

I waved my arm in the air. "Yes, yes, that's fine." I turned and repeated everything to Bellamy. He pressed his lips together. "Can you ask him who else might want to kill him?" Bellamy knew I'd asked that day, but in the shock and with the limited time, it had been a big ask of the newly deceased man.

I pivoted back to the ghost. "Do you know anyone, other than Joy, who'd want to kill you. Have you done anything to aggravate anyone lately?" While he thought about that, I looked back over my shoulder at Bellamy. "Maybe Chandler has an alias?"

"Maybe." The sergeant didn't look convinced. "Not going well with Mr Albertson?"

"Not yet." My eyes met Alan's again.

He scratched the back of his head, one hand on his hip. "Maybe two people? I mean, no one's ever threatened me, and honestly, these were minor things. Not something you'd murder someone over." He laughed nervously. "At least, I wouldn't kill someone over them."

"Oh. Who and what happened?" This didn't sound super promising, but maybe someone had overreacted about something. I took my notepad and pen out of my bag and readied myself.

"The first one was about a week before I was killed. I was driving along, and another car cut me off, so I beeped." He lifted his hands in front of himself and gesticulated. "Honestly, it was over nothing. I wanted him to know he'd done something dangerous. So he slammed the brakes on and blocked me. The person behind me almost ran up my arse. And this young guy with a shaved head and face tattoos gets out of his car and bangs on my window. He's shouting at me and threatening to punch my head in, so I pulled half onto the footpath and drove around him. I sped off because I was worried he'd try and run me off the road. I lost him, thank God."

"Oh, wow. That's nuts. Did you get his number plate?"

"No, but I can give you a good description. And he was driving an unforgettable car—an orange Aventador Lamborghini." Lucky he knew his cars. This was going to make Bellamy's job a lot easier.

I scribbled it all down. "That is unforgettable. Just a sec." I repeated everything to Bellamy.

He raised his eyebrows. "That's impressive, Miss Winters. No wonder you keep solving my cases. To be honest, I'm glad I know your big secret. I assumed you were either very lucky or a genius, and I was starting to worry about my own professional ability."

I smiled. "I have no doubt, Sergeant, that you would've solved every one of those crimes without me butting in. I just got there faster because I cheated." Not that it was my fault I could cheat, but Bellamy was an excellent policeman, and the last thing I wanted was for my ability to change how he felt about his own skills. This was another reason I could be glad I'd finally come clean to him. "So, Alan, who was the other person we should be chasing up?"

"There was a guy who invested money with the broking firm I work for. He was my client, and I lost some of his money." He looked up at the ceiling. *Right.*

"How much money, and how did you lose it?"

He licked his bottom lip and looked around. "Ah, about two hundred and twenty thousand." I tried to keep my face neutral, but boy, was that hard. I jotted it down. "He'd invested about three hundred with us. It was his whole retirement nest egg." He rubbed the back of his neck and finally met my eyes. "I felt terrible. I'd had a tip-off about a US tech company. They were doing okay… until they weren't. We lost the lot overnight."

How could he say "we" like he would suffer anywhere near as much as the guy he'd invested for. "Right. Did he ever threaten you?"

"No. He threatened to sue us, but he signed a waiver, and I invested after researching the company. It wasn't anything shady. It was just bad luck, and I don't have a crystal ball." He rubbed his chest.

"What was his name?"

"Alex Markovic. He lives in Exeter with his wife. They were recently retired… well, he isn't now." He winced, probably realising how bad that sounded.

I shook my head. "I don't know how you could sleep at night." Sometimes, I just had to say what I felt.

His eyes finally held remorse. "Sometimes I didn't. After that trade went wrong, I took stress leave for a week. Look, when people invest with us, they get to tick the box that tells us how risky they want to go. More risk can mean more return. He ticked the maximum risk. It wasn't like I was trying to lose his money. He could've ticked the lowest return, and we would've put it in bank stocks, a property fund, or even better-known tech with a dividend. He wouldn't have stood to make nearly enough, but it would've provided for a steady income most years."

I exhaled loudly. "Fair enough." I explained everything to Bellamy as I made more notes. "So, I guess you'll have to go through his work records, check all of it out." I wasn't going to say more than that. Bellamy knew how to keep going with the investigation. I might have had the luck, but he had all the experience.

"Thanks, Miss Winters."

I looked at Alan. "Anything else while I'm here? We probably won't be able to access your home again. Your sister will wonder what in Hades is going on."

He rolled his lips between his teeth and thought. "Hmm, no. That's about it."

"Okay. Thanks for your time today, Alan. We appreciate it."

"I guess I should thank you for trying to solve this. Um… how long have you been able to speak to ghosts?"

"About a year, give or take. Why?"

"Do you… do you know what happens now? I don't like just aimlessly floating around. I asked another ghost about it, and they said you can go to the darkness or the light, but they didn't know how. Is there anything else I should know?"

"I have no idea. What they said is correct, but how or why it happens and if there's a third choice—other than staying here as you are—I can't say. Good luck, though."

He gave an ironic laugh. "Yeah, thanks."

"Okay, Sergeant. We can go."

He looked in Alan's direction. "Thank you, Mr Albertson. We'll do our best to find your killer."

Alan shook his head. "I still think Joy did it, but you do you. Bye." He disappeared before I could say anything else.

I turned to Bellamy. "He said thanks and that he appreciates it." Imagine finding out the victim you're trying to get justice for didn't appreciate what you were doing. Sheesh. Bellamy's job was tough enough as it was. Although, even if Alan was ungrateful, if we could prove who really killed him, Joyless would be out of jail, and that would make Bellamy happy, so he still would've had motivation. "What now?"

"Now, I go back to the station and get my constables to pull all the information we need. I'll let you know when we have something."

"Is there anything I can do to help? I'll be writing an article on this when we're done, and the more involved I can be, the better. I'm sure our locals would love to know exactly how much work goes into your job, and that it's not always an easy path to catch the right crim." I also wanted to be involved because I was nosy, and it would be fun.

"How would you explain how we got from there to here? You can't exactly say you spoke to a spirit."

"No, but I'll figure that out when all's said and done. I can put in a little white lie, or I can leave some information out. I'm happy to have you read over it when it's finished." I gave him a hopeful look. "I help you; you help me."

He shut his eyes for a moment, then opened them. "I'm sure I'll live to regret this, but okay, Miss Winters. You can start by helping find these two people. Come on." He left the key on the counter and led the way out of the ungrateful ghost's home, so we could help another ungrateful person. But justice was justice. Also, I couldn't wait to see the look on Ironfist's face when Bellamy arrested his boss.

Revenge would be sweet.

CHAPTER 10

At the station, Sergeant Bellamy set me up at a spare desk, well, spare today only. "This is where PC Adams sits when she's not at the front desk. She said she's more than happy for you to use it for the next couple of hours. Patel has set you up with a special guest login." He pointed to a piece of paper next to the desktop computer. "You'll have access to the information you need for this case only, so don't even think of trying to sticky beak into other cases or files. I'd like you to search and get the details of all the orange Lamborghini owners in England of that model. There shouldn't be too many. Rank them in importance, beginning with the area the accident happened in, radiating outwards. If you need special permission for something you can't access, let me know. All the databases we use to search for people, car registration details, et cetera, you do have access to. I'll also know what you've searched, so don't go off script. And come see me when you're done with that. Am I understood?"

I smiled. "Yes, Sergeant. One hundred per cent."

He scrunched his face. "I hate that saying—100 per cent.

Why can't people just say yes? Such a waste of words." He turned and walked away. I promised myself that I would only say that to him when he was being extra annoying.

I grinned and sat in PC Adams's chair. The computer was on but asleep, so I pressed a key, and the screen brightened. How exciting! I was finally on the inside... deep inside. Finn would be so jealous. I'd text him and brag, but I had no reason as to why Bellamy would let me do this, so it was safer to say nothing. If he asked where I was later, I could just say that I tagged along to something small and newsworthy with Bellamy.

Bellamy must've mentioned what I'd be looking up because Patel had written down a couple of websites. One was the DVLA for the registration information. The other was a link to a file that contained all of Alan Albertson's email correspondence—both work and personal. That must be for later when I had permission to check out things for the guy who lost most of his retirement funds.

Okay, so this was fortuitous. The guy who cut Alan off could've driven a mini or a Toyota sedan or even a Peugeot, but thankfully, he was driving one of the rarest, flashiest cars in England... or anywhere, really. There were only thirty-eight orange Lambos in the whole of the UK. And how many of those were driven by a skinhead-looking dude? I'd wager not many.

I'd soon compiled a list of names, but only five of those were women. I didn't exclude them—in case a significant other had borrowed the car, or an adult child—but I did place them on an adjacent list on my spreadsheet, the closest addresses to the furthest away listed from one onwards. I printed it out and took the page to Bellamy.

"Good work, Winters." Ooh, we'd dropped the Miss. Maybe he was tired and forgot, or maybe he was finally getting used to me. "Are you sure you don't want to join the force?"

"No, Sergeant. Not this year, anyway. Ask me again next year or the year after, and I'll let you know." Okay, never say never. But I doubted that if I joined the force, I'd be allowed to work on many cases. They'd have me doing all the grunt work… arresting drunk and disorderly, doing traffic stops, that kind of stuff. It wasn't like they'd promote me to sergeant or detective after five minutes. I could do more good with my secret talent as things were, and this way, Bellamy would get most of the credit. I didn't care about the accolades—I'd be happy with making things right and with my paycheque from Julian.

"I'll get someone onto this now. If you'd like to go through the emails and flag all the correspondence with the client who lost his money, that would be helpful. Also, read all the emails and forward me the ones that have anything to do with that transaction and the client's dissatisfaction."

"Can do." I smiled and hurried back to Adams's desk. It took me forty minutes to sift through everything. At least finding the emails had been easy because I just searched the client's email address. Reading through them was torturous because three-quarters of them were just about what trades Alan was recommending and general chitchat. This man had been his client for three years, so there were even Christmas greetings and holiday notices. When I finished, I forwarded everything to Bellamy, and that was me done. All in all, there were seventeen emails back and forth about the disaster. The client had threatened to sue, as Alan had said, and one email said he'd love to show Alan how it felt to lose your retirement funds, but that was it. No death threats, or even threats of beating him up.

My heart was sore after reading the whole thing, though—

there were numerous mentions of how devastated he and his wife were, that they would both have to find work again after two years of retirement. I barely had £5,000 in the bank, let alone two hundred and fifty thousand, and I would feel sick to my stomach if someone stole the money, which was close to what happened. It was careless. It was a lesson—if I ever, ever had money to invest for the future, I would not tick the riskiest box. No siree.

I stopped in and said goodbye to Bellamy. "Thanks for letting me help. It was fun."

He looked at me as if I was crazy. "Only you would say that, Winters. My staff would be bored in five minutes going through that lot."

"Research is my jam. Half my job is research, and the other half is the interviews and writing. I love getting to the bottom of things. So, will you let me know what happens when you follow those up?"

His smile was kind. "Yes. You've been a huge help, and it's the least I can do. It shouldn't take too long. I've enlisted help from another station, and they're sending a couple of detectives to the car owners. I'll go and talk to the no-longer-retired client myself, either this afternoon or tomorrow morning."

"Sounds good. If I hear of anything else in the *ether*, I'll let you know."

"Yes, please. Bye, Miss Winters."

"Bye, Sergeant."

I drove straight to the pub because I'd finished later than anticipated, and I needed another coffee… and a piece of lemon meringue pie wouldn't be so bad either. The main area was half full, the lunch crowd slowly gathering. Meg was wiping down a table when I walked in. "Hey, gorgeous lady. How are you feeling today?"

"Oh, hey, Avery." She shrugged and gave a sad smile. "I'll live. What are you doing here?"

"I thought I'd check on my best friend, make sure she wasn't too upset about some loser guy who couldn't do better if he tried."

She fiddled with the cloth she'd used on the table. "You're too good to me."

I pulled a "you have to be kidding" face. "No way, chicky. It's what best friends do—check on their significant platonic other to make sure said *SPO* gets through things so she comes out the other side faster and is ready to have fun. It's purely selfish on my part. And I'm sure Carina would agree. Besides, I'm dying for a coffee and lemon meringue pie."

She chuckled, and that made me smile. "You're hilarious. But seriously, thank you. It means a lot that you care."

"A lot of people care about you… and we're the ones that matter." I winked. "Now, Bailey looks bored behind the counter. He's just waiting for someone to order coffee and dessert. I'll be back." I turned and made my way to the bar, warmth filling my chest. Again, I marvelled at what a difference having close friends made. I was the luckiest person ever. "Hey, Bails."

His wide smile still did things to my insides, but not as big as the things Finn's smiles did, which was redundant either way because I wasn't going to date either of them. "How are you? I've missed you around here."

"I've been busy, and last time I came in, you were on a date." I waggled my brows.

His smile turned into a grin. "Yeah, Stella and I went to dinner. It was her brother's birthday."

"Nice. So, could I order something?"

"No. This isn't a place to eat or drink. You'll have to go somewhere else." He pulled a silly face, his tongue sticking out.

"Ha ha, bite me." I laughed, then placed my order.

"Coming right up. Oh, and thanks for checking in on Meg. I know she hung out at yours last night, and I overheard what you said when you came in."

"It's my job as her friend, so no thanks needed." I gave him a wave and sat at a table next to the window—my favourite spot so I could people-watch both inside and out.

Meg placed meals on a table on the other side of the room, then rushed to the kitchen. She was soon back with two cappuccinos and my pie. She set my food and drink in front of me, and I inhaled the coffee scent. "Mmm, thank you. Just what I needed." I took a sip as she sat with the other coffee.

"Busy day?"

"Busy week. I'm helping Bellamy with a murder investigation on top of my normal articles and looking for a home for Zeus. I'm running on adrenaline at the moment."

"The case you're helping with wouldn't be Joyless's, would it?" Her stare was intense.

"Maybe."

Her mouth fell open. "You can't be trying to help her, surely? She's been so horrible to you." She knew that the case against her seemed open and shut, so there was no reason I would be helping unless it was to flip that around.

I shrugged. "She has, but there's doubt as to whether she did it." I had to give her some reason, so I gave her the truth with a bit of embellishment. "She was shocked when it happened, and she was upset. I don't think she's that good of an actor. If she doesn't like you, you know about it."

"But I heard she had motive. She owed him money."

"Yep, but there's doubt. He went there fairly regularly, and she tolerated him like she tolerates me. Why didn't she kill him before?"

"Because he wasn't asking for money?" She sipped her coffee.

"But how would she know he would ask on that particular day? I mean, she might have killed him"—I slipped that in there because I couldn't explain the whole ghost thing—"but there's reasonable doubt. Bellamy wants to prove it one way or the other, and they're short-staffed, so I offered to help."

"You're a good egg, Avery."

"Thanks." I gave her a cheesy grin, then tucked into my lemon dessert. Yum! My mouth exploded with saliva. This was sooooo delicious.

A woman was passing our table, and she stopped and looked down at me. Her shortish blonde hair was slicked back off her face with product, and she carried a Burberry bag and anger. So much rage in her eyes. Familiar eyes. "You!" She stabbed a red-polished talon towards me.

I looked around to see if there was someone behind me because I'd never seen this woman before. She looked familiar, but I was sure I'd never met her. Meg's eyes widened, and she parted her lips to speak when realisation hit me. "You're Joy's mother, aren't you?"

"That's right. And you're the cow of a journalist who refuses to help my sweet, helpless daughter on those trumped-up murder charges." Her voice rose with each word until the whole pub could hear over the soft music playing on the speakers. "She begged you… *begged* you! But you said you wouldn't help. I don't know how you sleep at night. I hope you choke on your cake." She swung around with the dramatics of a reality TV star in full rage mode and stalked off.

Meg and I stared at each other. Meg's forehead wrinkled. "I thought you said you were helping."

"I haven't told Joyless because I wanted her to stew for a while." I popped the last bit of lemony goodness into my mouth. Joyless's mother's anger had done nothing to ruin the taste, thank God.

Meg grinned. "Ha, she deserves to stew, too, and so does her witch of a mother."

"Seems like it. Also, does her mother know the Joyless we know? 'Sweet, helpless daughter' my behind."

"She's about as sweet and helpless as a crocodile." Meg placed her hand on mine. "Are you okay? That was a bit… much."

I took a deep breath. "Yeah, I'll be fine. Just another day in Crazybury." I sniggered.

"Hey, I resemble that!" Meg crossed her eyes.

"They really need to change the name. I might suggest it to the town organising committee next time I see them."

"I'll come with you. We'll have more luck as a team." She winked.

"Meg, sorry to bother you, but can we get a little help?" Her dad stood a few feet away, dirty plates in his hands. I waved at him, and he gave a nod.

"Yep." She stood. "Try to stay out of trouble."

"I'll do my best." I stood. "If you need anything, just let me know." I gave her a hug, waved bye to Bailey, and went out the back to Daisy. My phone rang. "Hey, Vinegar. What's up?"

"Hey. Someone's turned up to the office with no appointment to meet Zeus, and they seem to be getting along, and"—his voice lowered to a whisper—"they're completely normal."

I ignored the way my stomach plummeted. The word no was quickly shoved away, but oh, how I wanted to say it. "Um, wow. That's a good thing. Right?" I knew we needed to find him a home, but I wasn't ready to let him go. I didn't want to miss him.

"Are you asking me or yourself?"

The uncomfortable burn of tears raked my eyes. "You can't say yes to them yet. I'll be there in five minutes. Okay?"

"Are you crying, Lightning?" His voice was a mixture of surprise and kindness. If he made fun of me right now, he wasn't the person I thought he was.

"Not yet." Which was the truth. The tears hadn't slipped over onto my face yet.

"I'm sorry. I really am."

My voice was barely a whisper. "I know. Bye." I hung up before the wave of sadness swept me away. Talking was the door to crying. I had no idea why, but keeping my mouth shut made it easier to keep the moisture where it belonged—inside my body.

The office was basically around the corner and down the lane, so I was there quickly. I ignored the evil Bethany and jogged up the stairs. When I went inside the office, a gorgeous woman about my age, with shiny black hair down to her waist and huge brown eyes, stared down at Zeus.

"Hi," I said as I entered.

Finn waved towards me. "This is Avery. She put the ad in the paper."

"Hi, Avery, I'm Sylvia." And just like that, she opened her mouth and sucked in three short, quick breaths, then sneezed. And sneezed again, and again, and again. I grabbed a couple of tissues from the box on my desk and handed them to her. Her eyes watered, and she kept sneezing.

"Are you all right?" I wasn't sure if I expected her to answer through sneezes that kept coming or if I wanted her to know I cared.

"Oh—my—God. I think I—I—I, achoo!"

Zeus meowed and came to my feet. He stood on his hind legs and begged to be picked up, so I obliged, then took him to my desk and gave him a pat while Sylvia did her best to stop sneezing. After almost two minutes, she stopped, but her eyes were red and teary. "I'm so sorry. I was having shots for my cat allergy, but I don't think they're working. I haven't been near a cat for six months, so I didn't know."

Finn's shoulder's drooped, but I smiled and scratched under Zeus's waiting chin. "Looks like you're stuck with us for a little while longer, cutie pie." I kissed the top of his head.

"I'd better go. Sorry for wasting your time."

"Don't feel bad, Sylvia. I'm sorry you've had such a bad reaction. Thanks for trying." I wasn't going to be mean about it. She probably would've made a wonderful mum for Zeus. I knew I should be as disappointed as Finn, but maybe the universe would step in and find a way for one of us to keep him. Okay, so Finn just had to change his mind, but I had to move, which wasn't on the cards until my lease expired. "Hmm, maybe I could talk Josie into keeping him, and I'll offer to pay for all his food and vet bills and stuff, and I'll go over, give him cuddles and walk him."

He put his hands in his jeans pockets. "You really think she'd go for that?"

I hugged the cat tighter. "No. Not really, but I'm trying to stay positive."

Finn came over and patted Zeus, carefully avoiding touching my arm. Hmm, was I that much of a turn-off? "You could try and talk Mrs Collins into it."

"She's pretty disagreeable most of the time, and now is the worst time ever. If I pushed her, I don't know what she'd do."

His eyebrows drew down. "What do you mean? Why is it the worst time ever? What did you do?"

My lips widened into a smile in record time. "That's a fair question, but this one isn't my fault. Sort of. Okay, it's kind of my fault, but not in the way you think."

The door swung open, and I spun around. Carina strode

through the door, her magenta hair gloriously bright. "Hello, my sexy workmates. What's going on? Have you found a home for the wee one yet?" She shut the door behind her and came and patted Zeus, who had his happy face on. His eyes were shut, and he was smiling at all the attention.

Finn and I looked at each other. I sighed and said, "Unfortunately, the last person seemed fantastic, until she had a sneezing attack. She's allergic."

"Oh no! D'at's terrible."

Finn narrowed his eyes at me. "Yes, but Lightning isn't that upset by it. She's still trying to figure out how to keep him. Which is how we reached the conversation about Mrs Collins and why it's the worst time in the history of worst times for Lightning to be asking her about having a pet." He lowered his chin. "So, please continue with why it's your fault but not your fault."

Carina grinned. "Ooh, is this juicy gossip?"

She made me smile with her enthusiasm, but this wasn't a story to smile about, so I let it fade. "Don't you remember? I found the locket… her daughter's… her *missing* daughter's."

"It's sad but good, right?" asked Carina. "She couldn't be mad at you for finding it."

Zeus decided he'd had enough loving and jumped out of my arms. "Well, it's brought it all back for her, you know? And she never got closure."

Finn shook his head slowly. "That's horrific. No wonder she's so cranky with you."

Carina rolled her eyes. "She's grumpy with everyone and d'e situation, except you because you're so haaaaaaaandsome." She fluttered her eyelashes. I laughed.

"Whatever." He turned and went to his desk.

Carina grinned. "You can run, but you can't hide, Vinegar."

"I can work from home tomorrow. Would you both like that?"

"I'd be sad. Devo, in fact," I said. Carina's eyes bugged out, and Finn gave me a worried look. "Because then I wouldn't get to see Zeus."

Carina laughed. "You're so naughty, Avery."

"You wound me, fair maiden." Finn placed his palm on his heart.

The door swooshed open, and we all pivoted to see who it was.

Julian stepped inside and shut the door. Everyone was so diligent about keeping Zeus safe. What a bunch of good-hearted peeps. Julian's gaze roamed over us and finished on Zeus. "How's the adoption process going?"

Finn threw me a look before answering. "Not good. We nearly had someone this afternoon, until she almost died from her allergies."

"Oh, that's too bad." He tapped one foot on the floor. "I actually came in here to congratulate you all." He grinned. "We've won a prestigious award that acknowledges outstanding journalism within the community. This is the first time this office has ever won. I'm so proud of all of you." His eyes finally found me. "And we… or I should say Avery, has won a category all on her own."

My mouth dropped open. "No way! What?" Maybe it was a category for interviewing the craziest people?

Julian's eyes shone with what I assumed was pride. "You won the prize for best crime reporter. Your in-depth articles that outline the process and tie it in with the human story of the victims and their loved ones has caught everyone's attention."

The skin on my arms pebbled. "Is this for real? Like, it's not a joke?"

"I would never joke about something like this, Winters."

"Not to take away from the award of the whole team, but is it like a Devon-wide prize?" There was no way it was anything important. He hadn't even mentioned these awards before. No one here had.

"The prize is England-wide and given by the Sir Anthony Hedges Association of Journalists. They're the biggest journalism group in England. Sir Anthony Hedges used to be a big advocate for honesty and professionalism in our field, and he was bloody rich. Before he died, he set up this awards night and prize giving. You don't only get a trophy but a cash prize. The Manesbury Daily will get £20,000, and you'll get £10,000." While I had a mini heart attack at that amount—I had never, ever, ever won anything like that before—he looked at Carina and Finn. "Out of the prize the Manesbury Daily gets, I'd like to split it equally among you three and myself. How does that sound?"

Carina bit her bottom lip. "You mean, we get £5,000 each?"

"That's exactly what I'm saying. Good maths skills, Kelly."

It didn't seem fair that I got more than them. "I don't have to get the extra five. You can split it among you three." Okay, so I was nuts because I could always use more money—who couldn't—but they'd been here way longer than me, and it wasn't their fault that I could talk to ghosts. If it wasn't for that, I'd be less than average. I was a cheat and a faker. Which was fine before cash prizes were given because we all had our niches here. They were much better at their jobs than I was. But maybe one of them would've gotten the top prize if it wasn't for me, and if I wasn't here, they wouldn't have to share the other prize with me.

"Don't be ridiculous." Finn stood and stalked over. He looked down at me, his pretty blue eyes full of fire. "You, me,

C, Julian, we're the best team there is. Maybe we wouldn't have won it without you. Goodness knows we've never won it before."

"And you need d'e money. We don't feel hard done by at all, sweetie. I love d'at you won d'e od'er prize. You are amazing! You help the police solve crimes all d'e time, and you've put your life in danger doing it."

"And Vinegar's," I pointed out, because it would be rude not to.

"Yes," he said, "and I'm getting some money. If you feel guilty, buy me dinner one night, now you're all cashed up." He grinned, his dimples showing. That was cruel. Maybe that was my punishment—buying a hot guy dinner and having to stay friends. The universe was definitely having a laugh at my expense.

Julian clapped, and I jumped. "Now, team. No more arguing about who gets what. Everyone is getting what they deserve, and I'm equally proud of all of you. The event is in two weeks, which isn't a lot of notice, but it's black tie in London, and tickets for nominees are given gratis by the organisers. I've arranged a limo to pick us all up from here. My wife is attending, but I'm sorry that you can't bring a plus one. I hope that's okay."

Finn held his hands up. "No problems here."

"Nor me," said Carina.

"I'll be single till I die, probably, so I'm all good too. Maybe someone can FaceTime Meg for the exciting parts."

"Ooh, good idea, Avery. She'll love d'at."

"Right, squad. Get those outfits ready. It's a date!" Julian rubbed his hands together, turned, and left.

We all looked at each other, our grins nearly identical in hugeness. I couldn't believe I'd won all that money. That was crazy. I wasn't going to squeal about it here because it felt like I was showing off or something, but I was totally squealing into my pillow when I got home—Mrs Crabby wouldn't enjoy listening to me scream in joy.

"I can't wait!" Carina was hopping from foot to foot, vibrating with excitement.

"It's going to be the best night." Finn didn't often get excited about things. He was more of a smooth operator. "Free booze!"

I laughed. "Ah, that makes sense as to your excitement level."

"The money's not a bad reason, either, and the free limo." Finn's grin lost a few points of wattage. "I've worked with Julian for a few years now, and he's a good guy and a great boss. He deserves this just as much as we do. I can't wait."

What a rollercoaster of a week. One minute I was up, then down, then up again. My gaze found Zeus. And there was the down part. If only I knew how to make it an up. Why were other people's problems easier to solve than your own?

CHAPTER 11

The next morning, I went for my usual walk and tried not to think obsessively about the fact that Josie said no to my idea of her having Zeus for the foreseeable future, with me paying for him. Today was handover day from Finn to her. She had agreed to three weeks with the cat, but that was it. I didn't even know why I'd bothered. Three weeks wasn't enough time for me to let my lease expire and find somewhere else. And there was no way Mrs Crabby was going to say yes to a pet. I was just prolonging my own agony. By the time the right person showed up for Zeus—and I had little doubt they would in three weeks—I'd be even more attached.

When I reached the place I'd found the locket, I turned to head back, and so did my thoughts. Why didn't Everly want her murder solved? She hadn't wanted to upset her mother, but that was done now. Mrs Crabby was revisiting that time, and she wasn't coping. I'd checked on her when I'd come home last night, and she'd thanked me, then shut the door. No venom, no lectures, just meh. I had a feeling she was depressed. And who could blame her?

Hadn't Everly had enough time to come to terms with being murdered? Maybe her counselling others was because she wanted to keep herself busy so she didn't have to confront her own issues. If it were me, I'd want to see that person burn in hell. I'd want the law to squish them like someone toeing out a cigarette on the ground. Smoosh them so hard, it shredded them into minuscule pieces.

Why didn't she want justice?

She said it wasn't her mother, but maybe it was someone else she loved.

I sucked in a quick breath. Could that be it? Did she not hate the person who'd killed her, and she didn't wish them ill?

I hoped not. Had she been lured in by a psychopathic narcissist? Had the manipulation of her thought process kept hold of her all these years?

As soon as I was safely inside my apartment, I called out to her—not loudly, of course. I didn't want Mrs Crabby to hear. Everly appeared. She smiled. "Hey, Avery. What's up?"

"Hey. I was just thinking…. I don't want to upset you, but I have a question."

She folded her arms. "It sounds like you actually don't care if you upset me because I bet you still ask the question."

I looked at the ground for a moment. She had me there, but I did care. I met her gaze, her face stern and closed off. Chances were not good that she'd answer me. "Did you love the person who killed you? Is that why you don't want justice?"

Something in her expression eased. "No. I didn't love my murderer. Is that it because I have things to do?"

I put my hands behind my back and crossed my fingers. "Who killed you, Everly? Where is your body?" I'd learned a lot about ghosts in the last few months, and I was pretty sure she'd be able to find her body because ghosts were initially drawn to where they lived and the place they died, and where their body was. "Please tell me. You'd give your mum closure. She needs that."

Tears glossed her eyes, and she shook her head. "I can't, Avery. I'm sorry." She disappeared.

What in Hades was stopping her? Was her killer dead and threatening her somehow? Were they a poltergeist? Argh, so many questions.

My phone vibrated—I always turned it onto silent at night, and I hadn't turned it back yet. I grabbed it from the pocket in my workout tights. That invention had finally brought women's sportswear into the modern age. I was surprised by the name on the screen—it was only eight thirty. "Hello, Sergeant. Have you got news?"

"Yes, but it's not exciting. It does move us forward, just not in a good way."

Okay, that sounded like a roundabout way of saying it wasn't good news. "Hit me."

"I spoke to the man whose life savings are gone, and he's been away in Spain, staying with his daughter for the last three weeks. There's no way he could've orchestrated it. We've checked his phone records, and there's been no calls to anyone in England, let alone a Mr Chandler. He also sounded quite shocked when we told him that Alan was dead. So he has an alibi, and we can't connect him to anyone unusual. There's been no large payments from his bank account to anyone, nor have there been any large cash withdrawals. My gut—and all the evidence—says he's innocent."

"Oh, okay. We still have the Lambo driver to question, don't we?"

"About that. We found the driver. After that altercation, they had nothing to do with Alan. They were actually down here from Leeds on business. Again, they have an alibi for the two days before and the morning Alan was murdered. They've been at work in Leeds the whole time. We also have them on a Zoom call from home to Italy at 11-11:45 p.m. the night before he was killed. We've checked their bank details and phone records. Nothing. They've been enormously accommodating by answering our questions and giving us access to everything."

"Right." I sighed. "So, where does that leave us?" Why I even asked, I had no idea. I knew where it left us. With a big, fat nothing.

"Back to the beginning. Are you sure that ghost isn't playing you?"

"No. And to what end?"

"I don't know, Winters."

Had Joyless done it, and *she* was playing us? She was a liar and a prickly person. It wasn't out of the question she'd done it, despite what her mother thought. Hmm…. My next suggestion would put me in the firing line, but I had nothing to hide, so I didn't care. "Maybe we're looking at this all wrong?"

His tone was curious. "How so?"

"Maybe she was set up. Maybe it's not about Alan at all but about her. Could someone have killed him because it would make her look bad, or was it random? Manesbury isn't known for its forward-thinking residents. Most people here are traditional. We could ask Anna how much almond milk they go through compared to cow's milk, or even oat milk. Get a breakdown of milk popularity. Maybe Alan was just collateral damage?" How had I not considered this before? "How come you guys didn't think of this?" *Oops.* It was out of my mouth before I could stop it. *Stupid mouth.*

"We did consider it. We asked Miss Stick if she had any enemies, if anyone would want to frame her. She said there's been no threats against her and that no one hated her."

I laughed. How could I not? "Sergeant, I hate her… not

enough to kill someone to frame her, and you can go through my phone records and bank accounts, whatever. But she's a horrible person when she wants to be, and that's a hundred per cent of the time with me and probably with a few other people. Surely I'm not the only person she's bullied for no good reason."

I heard someone call his name in the background. "I don't know what to say, Winters. I'll think about it. I have to go. We'll talk about this later. Bye."

He hung up without giving me a chance to farewell him. Whatever. Why was nothing going my way? Maybe I'd run out of luck. Things had been ticking along fairly well for me lately —awesome friends, solving crimes, winning journalism prizes. My stomach flipped at the last one. But in the last few days, more things than usual were going wrong—finding a place for Zeus, Meg's breakup, this investigation, Everly's locket. Maybe I should just give up on helping Joyless. Maybe Bellamy was right, and that ghost was just steering me wrong for fun.

The only way I could see reaching the truth was to discover who Mr Chandler was. There was another way to possibly find information, and that would be to interview everyone in Manesbury about their feelings on Joyless. And that would be a stupidly long process. By the time I was done, she'd have gone to trial and be in jail. Not that that was an issue if she was guilty. But what if she wasn't? My view on this was seesawing from one hour to the next, which meant I wasn't sure, which also meant I needed to keep digging until I was.

I hated myself for being this willing to help someone who hated me, but my need for justice was stronger than my need for petty revenge. As horrible to me as she was, the time she'd already spent in jail was probably recompense enough, at least for my wounds.

"Charles, can you come over? Charles?"

After thirty seconds, his voice came from outside the front door. "Hey." He slid through, plonked on the couch, and looked up at me. "What's up?"

"I need more help with Mr Chandler and Ironfist. The investigation has run aground, and the only way we'll refloat it is if we find out who Chandler is. I don't know if Joyless killed Alan or not, to be honest. And if she didn't do it, the physical evidence and witnesses, including me, will get her put away." I couldn't tell the court I'd seen a ghost… well, two ghosts, on the day. What I did recount would help put Joyless in jail.

"I don't know how else I can help. I don't know where else Ironfist hangs out. Could you try talking to him again?"

When I thought of how much I goaded him…. "Um, no. I pretty much burned that bridge to nanoparticles." I walked to the window and stared across at Josie's house. Finn was dropping Zeus there this afternoon. I turned back to look at Charles because wandering thoughts weren't going to help. "There must be some way." I thought for a moment. "Hmm, could we send someone undercover?"

Charles pursed his lips. "What do you mean? A ghost or a live person?"

"Either. Could you go undercover, pretend you were looking for him before because you heard how awesome their gang was and you wanted to join? Maybe you could pretend your dad was your idol, and you want to follow in his footsteps."

Sadness, fear, and rejection all flared in his eyes. He kicked at the couch with his heels, but his legs swung straight through. "I don't know if I can do it." His soft voice hit me straight in the heart.

I returned to the couch and sat next to him. "I'm sorry to

ask and to phrase it that way, but it could help. *You* could help. Those ghosts can't hurt you, can they?"

He shrugged. "I don't know. Maybe a little, but probably not too much. They're scary, though. And I… I hate my dad. I hate what he did." Anger crept around the edge of his words.

His pain bled through. What he didn't say was loud and clear—I loved my dad. How could he have treated me like that? I vibrated an out breath like a horse making a noise, reminding myself of the identifies-as-a-horse Carly. "I know, Charles. It hurts when they behave badly, when they're not the parents we deserve—because make no mistake, and I know you know this, but it bears repeating: we are awesome, and they are horse excrement. But maybe we can use that experience for good. I don't know if Joyless killed Alan, but I have a small amount of doubt. That means we need to try. Imagine if we find out in years to come, after she's rotted in jail, that she didn't kill him? She's horrible, but even I can admit that in that case, she wouldn't deserve to be there. Do you want that on your conscience? I don't." I was such a meanie, putting this on a kid, even if he'd existed way longer than me.

He scratched his thigh. "I don't, but…" He hung his head, and I gave him space to think. Eventually he lifted his head and met my gaze. "What about if we get Sergeant Fox to find someone? He knows many ghosts, some of them criminals from when he was a policeman. He has a couple of petty crims that he helped go straight. They would probably go undercover if he asked."

"That's a good idea if they have no connection to those other crims." I allowed myself a small smile. "That could actually work."

He stood, his movements more energetic. Relief spread through my veins like a warm tide. He was okay. "I'll let you know how I go. Bye, Avery."

"Bye." I gave him a wave, and then he was gone. Before I could take a breath and consider all the new developments this morning, my phone rang. The mobile number on the screen wasn't one I recognised. "Hello, Avery Winters speaking."

"Hello, it's Mavis Holstead. I was wondering if you're coming to our appointment. You're half an hour late." Her annoyed tone was unmissable. She'd managed to put some force behind it. Obviously an old pro… at being annoyed. I snickered to myself and looked at my phone quickly to check the time before placing it against my ear.

"I'm sorry, Ms Holstead, but I have our appointment marked down for nine thirty. It's nine now."

"It's not nine now. It's nine thirty."

I closed my eyes and counted to five. "What clock have you checked on?"

"My kitchen clock. It hasn't lost a minute in fifteen years."

"My phone clock says it's only nine, but I can be there in ten minutes. Is that okay?" I wasn't going to win this argument. Bull-headed stubbornness with a side of ignorance was winning against logic, and far be it for me to try and stand in its way.

"Fine, but I hate waiting. You've messed up my whole morning. Don't dawdle. Goodbye."

"Bye."

I hurriedly showered and threw on my black trousers, flat, black boots, and a fitted, black turtleneck jumper. Today I was feeling the heaviness. If I was going to have to fight through the day like a badass, I was going to dress like one.

The morning was crisp and cool, the sun shone, and Mavis Holstead lived only a mile down the road. I'd rather have walked, but because I was "running late," I drove. The ridiculousness of some people was next level, but I had no spoons left this morning to force reality on someone who was clearly delusional. Hmm, and wasn't that an oxymoron?

I pulled into the short driveway of a two-storey, semi-detached stone house. The house was pretty enough, but there was nothing special about the garden. There was grass edged meticulously so that none of it grew over the stone path that led to the small front porch. No flowers or shrubs sprouted anywhere. The overall impression was neat minimalism.

I knocked on the door and stared down at the small, unexpected splash of red and green. A garden gnome sat to the right of the doorway. Rather than worn and maybe a bit dirty from being outside, he was shiny and clean.

The door opened. A woman about my height and in her sixties stood there. Her dark brown hair was pulled back in a chignon. Her white blouse and knee-length taupe skirt were ironed to perfection. "Glad you could finally make it, Avery."

I looked at my phone. "Yes, me too. Getting this over and done with early was actually a great idea." I smiled. If she wanted to have a sarcastic conversation, I was here for it.

Her mouth opened slightly before closing and opening again. "Please, come in."

I smiled and entered the hallway. She shut the door, overtook me, and went through a doorway to the left. Two padded recliners sat facing a small TV, and a pot-belly stove sat in one corner. The low ceiling gave me a sense of claustrophobia, but this overly cosy room was a snug, a room that was common here but something we didn't have in Australia. I figured it was because our climate didn't get cold enough for anyone to shut themselves into a small, easy-to-heat room.

She put her hands on her hips and looked at me. "So, as you know, I wanted to complain about the terrible job that Bartlet's Painters did. Here is exhibit A." She pointed to the section of wall just above the skirting board. "It's bubbling, and that bit's peeling. It hasn't even been fourteen months. I called them, and they came and looked."

I had my pad and pen out. "And what did they say?" I had a feeling I knew what they'd said—the house needed damp-proofing, and it wasn't their fault.

She repeated what I'd thought. "But I looked it up on the internet, and it's because they didn't prepare the wall properly."

I studied the wall from the skirting up. The paintwork was smooth. There were no settlement cracks either. They'd obviously sanded and plastered whatever needed it. I took a photo of the damp and the good wall. I turned my attention back to Mavis. I didn't want to weigh in on what had happened, considering I wasn't an expert, so I kept my opinion to myself. I just wasn't going to publish this piece. Another waste of time. Yay me. And this week's theme of "let's stuff Avery up" continued. "So, what are you going to do now?"

"Oh, I'm not finished yet. Come upstairs." It wasn't a request, so I wasted more of my day and followed her up. She led me to a bedroom at the back and pointed to the ceiling near the cornice and stared up at it. "Look at that water stain. They didn't use enough paint, and it's come through again. And they must have used really thin paint. Not enough coats at all. I can't believe I paid for that." She turned to me. "It's unacceptable. I've been ripped off!" Her face became a maelstrom of outrage. "I want their business shut down. Your article needs to out them to everyone. I need to warn the people, my fellow community members."

I wasn't game to say anything, but that water stain was obviously because she had a leak from her roof, and it hadn't been fixed. Should I say something now, or should I slink away quietly and just not write the article and blame it on Julian when she calls to complain? Maybe she could complain about the painters and the useless journalist to another journalist. I rolled my lips into my mouth to keep from smiling. I cleared my throat. "I'm not sure because I'm not an expert, but I think you have a leak in your roof. Have you had anyone come and look at it?"

Her eyes widened. "You don't believe me?"

"Um, it's not that I don't believe you believe what you're saying. I know you stand by your comments 100 per cent."

"Indeed I do. And you should too. I'd hate to complain about you to your boss."

"I'm sure you would." I managed to wring all the sincerity out of that comment that I could. I deserved an Academy Award. "You seem like the sort of person who hates to complain."

She eyed me for a while, likely assessing whether I was being sarcastic or not. See how good I was? Finally, she folded her arms. "Why haven't you taken a photo of the bad paint job?"

"I was saving that for the end. Taking photos is my favourite part, but I'll do it now." I took a picture of the water damage, and I was happy to. I could show Carina and Finn later, and we could all laugh about it.

"And when is this going to be in the paper? Tomorrow at the latest, I hope."

"Well, that's up to my boss. He gets the final say on what articles make it in and what don't." *And yours won't, but you won't be able to blame me.* Many people complained about their boss, and it was true that sometimes bosses could be painful; however, at times like this, I loved having a boss to pass the responsibility and blame to. It was a weight off my shoulders. This stress was above my pay grade.

"Well, you let Mr MacPherson know that I'll be more than disappointed if this doesn't make it in. Those painters are a menace. They'll leave wrack and ruin all over the county if they're not stopped."

I held in my sigh. "I'll be sure to let him know." I glanced at my phone. "Oh, look at the time."

Her brows drew down. "What time is it?"

"It's nine thirty." *The time I was supposed to get here.*

"It can't be. You didn't get here until way after that. It must be ten." I showed her my phone screen. "Well, Avery, complain to the phone company. They've got it wrong." She huffed. "I don't know why it's my job to correct everyone all the time. It's tiring. As if I don't have enough to do."

I smiled because what else could I do? "I'll be sure to email Apple and tell them they don't know what they're doing."

"Good. Also tell Mr MacPherson that I want the front page, page two at a pinch."

I coughed my laugh out. "Ah, yeah, sure, Ms Holstead. Have a lovely day." That was a great phrase when you wanted out of a conversation and you couldn't afford to get fired. Without waiting for her response, I hurried out and down the stairs. I opened the door and threw a "Goodbye" over my shoulder, and then I was out of there, hopefully never to return. The way I practically ran, it was as if a ghost was chasing me.

For a change, it wasn't.

CHAPTER 12

Back in the office, I went straight to Julian's office and explained the situation with Mavis. He agreed that we didn't want a libel case on our hands and told me not to write the article. "Don't worry. If she calls, I'll handle it." He chuckled.

"What? Do you enjoy fending off annoyed people? You do know she'll probably go to another paper and complain about us." I grinned.

"I've dealt with her before… a few times." He leaned back in his chair and tapped his pen on his thigh. "She calls us about three times a year to complain about local businesses. We only went with her story once, when it was warranted. She got some local firm to do her roofing, and it leaked. They went into liquidation after that anyway—too many unhappy customers."

I gasped. "So she knew her roof was leaking yet tried to blame the painters. What a galah."

Julian gave me a curious look. "Isn't that a parrot?"

"Yes. It's a pink one. There's lots where I live. It's a saying… like, what a fool."

His eyes squinted with a huge smile. "That she is." He flew forward and slapped his hands on the desk. "So, is that all?"

I jumped. "Ah, yes." After calming myself enough to stand without toppling the chair, I stood. "Have a good day."

"You too, Winters."

Before I'd even left, he'd picked up his phone and was calling someone. He was always such a flurry of energy and activity it made me tired. Maybe he was taking some of my energy to replenish himself. Did that make him some kind of paranormal being? I laughed to myself. Nope, not going there. I had enough on my plate with ghosts. My sanity didn't need me to imagine what else there was in the world that I had no idea about. I was happy to remain ignorant.

I went into my shared office. Carina and Finn were out, and Zeus was probably with Finn or at his flat. The handover to Josie was this afternoon. I pouted. It wasn't fair. I was going to miss him. Why couldn't I have a cat? I looked at the floor, considering whether I had time for a quick tantrum.

My phone rang.

Nope. No tantrum for me today. Damn it.

"Hello, Sergeant. I wasn't expecting to hear from you for a while." Not after this morning's unhappy conversation.

"Well, I thought you might want to hear about the milk situation at Heavenly Brew."

I placed my bag on my desk and sat. "Yes, please. How popular is almond milk?"

"Not very, but then again, popular enough. The majority of milk they sell is cow's milk, followed by oat milk, soy, and lastly almond. They sell two to four cups of almond-milk coffee a day."

"So, if they wanted her to go to jail, they'd have more

chance with someone the police could prove she was having trouble with. It would've been easier to kill a normal-milk person, but then where would the motive be… unless it was me. Then the motive would've been clear." Had I just dodged a coffee-cup-shaped bullet? Maybe I could've been the intended victim but because I'd been avoiding Heavenly Brew unless I was desperate, it made it difficult. A shiver scurried down my spine.

"I wasn't going to go there, but you said it. Anyway, I'd like you to come in and discuss it with me. I want to show you something, and maybe you'll be able to help."

I sensed a busy afternoon in my immediate future. "Sure thing. I'll come down now. I do have a question, which brings us back to our original reason, probably the biggest one that makes her look guilty—how did they manage to target him? How could they know he'd be there then and be served before someone else who wanted almond milk?"

"Well, that ghost was probably spying on Alan. They do that, don't they? They sneak around here and watch me."

I bit my tongue so I wouldn't laugh at the put-out tone of his voice. I couldn't blame him for feeling creeped out or uncomfortable. "Ah, yes, they do. But a human would've had to plant the poison. A ghost wouldn't have enough power, for want of a better word, to move a full carton of almond milk, or put the poison in it."

"Well, let's assume the ghost was watching Alan and overheard him telling someone he was going down there to ask for his money and grab a coffee. We can hypothesise the rest when you get here."

I felt like we were really stretching things. The timing had to be perfect, or she would've killed the wrong person. And I could see Alan telling someone he was going to tell her he wanted his money, but would he bother saying he was getting a coffee? Although, maybe they could assume it since he some-times got coffee from there. I shut my eyes and took a few deep breaths. Was I wasting more time following a path that was unlikely? Hopefully, Fox would have some news about his guys going undercover for us when I went in, and I could pass it on to Bellamy. Having insiders in the gang would make it way easier to find this Mr Chandler. "Sure thing. See you soon. Bye, Sergeant."

"Bye, Winters."

As I walked past reception on my way out, one word floated from Bethany's area. "Slag." It wasn't loud enough to be super clear, but it was loud enough to have me stopping and narrowing my eyes. She said it. I was sure she did. My heart pounded as I listened hard to see if she said anything else. Should I say something? She'd probably deny it with a sly look on her face. I could do without the confrontation. I swallowed and started walking. If she did it again, I'd have a word. If she denied it, she'd know she not only upset me but she'd gotten away with it because what was I going to do? Tell the boss without actual proof? I'd end up looking like a paranoid whinger, especially after the "altercation" we'd had in front of Julian over the cat. He'd think I was trying to get back at her.

The door closed behind me as I stepped onto the street, and I breathed out my annoyance. Karma would get her one day just as it had gotten her sister. These people could be horrible for only so long before they trod on the wrong tail. Which led me to another thought. If we assumed that Joyless wasn't framed, was she stupid enough to think she'd get away with it in such obvious circumstances? I'd have to bring that up with Bellamy too. Not that I thought she was a genius—far from it—but how stupid would you have to be?

PC Adams was manning the front desk when I went in. She took in me and my handbag. "No tart? Where's my tart?"

I gave a small laugh. "Oops. My bad. To be fair, I said within two weeks. It hasn't been that long."

"Hmm, okay. I'll let you off… for now. But I'm watching you." She narrowed her eyes, but her lips twitched as she held in a smile.

I wiped the back of my hand across my forehead. "Phew! Don't worry, I haven't forgotten. Your tart is coming."

The door buzzed. "Right answer. You've earned entry into the inner sanctum."

I giggled. "That sounds kind of rude."

She laughed and waggled her brows. "The sergeant's waiting for you. Have fun."

"Ha, heaps of it. See you later."

She waved as I pushed the door open and entered the hallway. In the main office area, Patel and PC Falkner—the young constable I'd only recently met—were standing together in the middle of a game of rock-paper-scissors. Patel threw rock, Falkner scissors. His shoulders slumped, and Patel grinned, patting him on the back. "Bad luck, mate. Off you go."

I eyed them. "What happens to the loser?"

Falkner shook his head and walked off towards the bathroom. Patel's cheeky grin grew bigger. "Someone made a mess in the bathroom, and the cleaners aren't back until tonight. He drew the short straw."

I shuddered. "Ew. I'm sorry I asked."

He shrugged, and I kept going. Bellamy's door was open a few inches. I was about to announce myself when I noticed two young women in the guest chairs. Bellamy hadn't seen me yet either, so I decided to eavesdrop and see if it was okay for me to knock.

"What's going to happen to her now?" the blonde one asked.

"She'll stay here another week before being transferred to a prison where she'll await trial."

The women grabbed each other's hands. The brunette said, "But she didn't do it. She said so, and I can't believe she would. Isn't that right, Camilla?" The blonde nodded. "She's not doing well in there. Maybe you could let her out for good behaviour or something."

Sergeant Bellamy's hands were linked on the table. He looked down at them and cleared his throat, probably trying to compose himself. Joyless obviously chose friends she could be smarter than. It probably made her feel better about herself. "I'm afraid it doesn't work like that."

The brunette's voice wobbled, as if she was about to cry. "But she still loved Alan. She told everyone she broke up with him, but she swore me to secrecy—he broke up with her. She wanted to get him back." That's not what I saw at the café. Joyless had been angry, and I doubted she was capable of loving anyone but herself. If she'd wanted him back, surely she would've been nicer to him. The brunette turned to the blonde. "Isn't that right, Camilla? She still loved Alan."

I could only see the women side-on, but I had enough of a visual to notice the blonde's jaw bunch for a moment. She sighed dramatically. "I don't know. She didn't confide in me like she confided in you." Maybe she was upset that she was lower down the friend food chain than the brunette. "But it's possible, yes." She jerked straighter in her chair. "Ooh, I know, maybe it was a crime of passion? You know she gets worked up about stuff sometimes, Lisa. How romantic."

Bellamy openly stared, disbelief in his eyes. "Romantic?"

She smiled. "Yes! She loved him so much but didn't want anyone else to have him. I wish someone loved me like that."

The brunette nodded and gave her a sincere look. "I think Paul loves you like that."

Camilla did a dismissive hand-wave thing. "Oh, I don't know about that. He has said he loves me, but is it 'to kill for' love? I don't know yet."

Bellamy peered at the women, his face a mask of politeness, but his eyes told a different story. He looked haunted, like he'd just discovered human intelligence didn't exist and that he was a cyborg. "Ahem, ladies." They simultaneously swivelled their heads to look at him. "I think we're getting off track. You wanted to know if she could get out early, and I'm afraid not."

The brunette folded her arms. "I can't believe it. She didn't do it. You know she didn't, Sergeant."

"I'm afraid I know nothing of the sort."

Camilla pouted. "But she loved him. You should've seen her face when she told me he was coming in to see her. You can't fake that emotion. It was love, not anger or hate in her eyes. She would never kill him."

Bellamy's eyebrows rose ever so slightly as he tried not to let it show that that was news to him. I, however, was in stealth mode, and I let my mouth drop open. Joyless knew he was coming in? That changed things. I thought back to that day. She hadn't looked like someone who was pleased to see him, but did that mean anything? I'd gotten there too late to know if she'd seemed surprised when he first came in. The sergeant relaxed his face and put on a calm voice. "Did Alan email her or call about coming in?"

The friend shrugged. "She didn't say. He might have even done it on social media or via another friend. Apparently he sometimes got hold of her that way when she refused to talk to him." That made sense since he'd been chasing her for money. I'd bet that she could make herself scarce when she wanted to. If only she owed me money.

"What are you doing here?"

I jumped and only just managed not to gasp out loud.

Goosebumps ran along my arms and the back of my neck. Ironfist stood there, his snide expression menacing. Patel looked at me from across the room. I smiled and gave him an "I'm okay" wave. I couldn't even answer the ghost. Damn it.

"Eavesdropping where you shouldn't be? Tut, tut, tut."

There was so much I wanted to say—like why was he here and to go to hell—but Patel would have me committed. So I ignored my instincts that said not to and turned my back on Ironfist in dismissal. He must've touched me because ice stabbed between my shoulder blades. I sucked in a breath, fought the urge to run into Bellamy's office, and knocked on the door.

"Come in."

I stepped in and acted surprised to see the two women. I smiled. "Hi." The ladies peered at me as if they were trying to work something out. Joyless had probably shown them a picture of me or something and told them how much she hated me. I turned to Bellamy. "Hello, Sergeant. I didn't realise you were in a meeting."

"These ladies are Miss Stick's friends. They just visited her and wanted to know how the case was going."

"Ah, right." I wasn't sure what he wanted me to say. Should I commiserate with the women about what a shame it was that Joyless might be in jail for the next twenty years? The news would surely get back to her. Was I that cruel? Yes. "It's such a sh—"

"Aren't you the one Joy posted about on Facebook?" Camilla peered at me through her long fake lashes.

I assumed an expression of non-botherment. "You're observant." Wow, sarcasm was my language of the day. But was it my fault if the universe put morons in my way?

She narrowed her eyes. "You were there!" She pointed a manicured finger at my chest.

I played dumb. "There where?"

Creepy Ironfist had materialised and was eagerly watching the show.

"You were there, in the café when Alan died. You could've done it. You hated Joy. And Joy doesn't know why. What did she ever do to you?"

I blinked. "Several things, actually, but I arrived when she was already making the deadly drink, so I have no idea how you think I had anything to do with it." Was that a flash of sympathy in her eyes? If it was, it was there and gone in a nanosecond, so wishful thinking I had probably imagined it.

Bellamy stood. "Okay, ladies. I have a meeting with Miss Winters now, so I'll have to ask you to leave."

They stood. Lisa smoothed a hand down her black jacket, and Camilla elegantly lifted the black-and-gold chain-link strap of her Chanel handbag over her shoulder. Joy hung out with some upmarket people, but they had the same down-market brains. The women said goodbye and left. When they shut the door, I sat in one of the chairs and glared at Ironfist. "Oh no, poor reporter wants to say something to me, but she can't. Not so tough now, are you?"

I looked at Bellamy. "Excuse me for one moment, Sergeant." I stood toe to toe with Ironfist and smiled, making sure to show some teeth. His confident expression wavered. "Oh, I'm still tough, loser. Why are you skulking around the police station?" I looked around. "Oh, you're trying to spy while Sergeant Fox isn't here." The widening of his eyes indicated I'd hit the mark. "Sergeant Fox, are you around? Sergeant Fox?" Doing all this in front of Bellamy while Ironfist was here was stupid of me. I should've thought before I reacted because now Ironfist knew that Bellamy knew my secret. There was no other explanation for the way I was behaving in front of the sergeant. He would probably pass that information onto Chandler, and now they'd be warier.

The ghost appeared next to me. "What's up, Mi—" He noticed Ironfist. "Get out of my station."

"There's no point spying now. We're not going to talk about anything important while you're here."

Ironfist stuck his fist up. "Want a walloping?"

Sergeant Fox shook his head, a calm police countenance on his face. "I'm only going to say it one more time. Leave. My. Station." Other than the cold, I'd never felt Fox's presence, but it was as if the air pressure changed. I held my breath. It was like the calm before the storm. Ironfist paled slightly and swore. After a few beats, he decided to do the smart thing and left.

I let out the air in my lungs. "Thank you, Sergeant Fox. That was impressive. I didn't know you could do that." Not that he'd done much, but I had a feeling he had more secrets than I could guess.

He smiled. "My pleasure, Miss Winters. Also, I have a couple of my men on that case you spoke to Charles about."

"Thank you so much. I appreciate it. Please let me know when you have some information."

"Of course. Now, if you'll excuse me, I was in the middle of something. Goodbye, Miss Winters."

"Bye, Sergeant."

He disappeared, and I sat. Bellamy massaged his temples. "I don't know if I'll ever get used to that. What happened?"

I told him, then said, "I could ask you the same thing about Joy's friends. They were… ditzy. Fancy thinking killing someone is romantic." I shuddered. A blush crept along my cheeks at the look on Bellamy's face. "Ah, yeah, I was standing outside listening for a bit."

He chuckled. "Well, saves me explaining things to you."

He shook his head. "Her take on romance was a worry, but that other piece of information was rather interesting, was it not?"

"The bit about her knowing he was coming? Very interesting. Did you go through her phone records or emails before you arrested her?"

"We did when she denied knowing he was going to see her. We also went through her computer and iPad, looking for anything to do with poisons, how to kill someone, and where to buy cyanide. We found nothing, and she hadn't wiped her search history. It was all there, everything from the last couple of years."

"But there's the private window search you can do, right?"

"Yes, but we engaged a digital forensic expert. They can find what websites you've visited and any hidden files you may have downloaded. He found no evidence of anything, which is another reason I'm sceptical about her guilt. On the surface, she's guilty, but my gut is telling me something's off." He sighed.

"Well, I might be able to help. I've had Sergeant Fox—"

"The ghost who hangs out here?"

"Yes. I've had him recruit ghost cons that turned onto the straight and narrow under his influence when they were all alive. A couple of them have agreed to…"—I looked around to make sure Ironfist hadn't snuck up on us again, and I lowered my voice—"go undercover with that gang, see if they can find out who Mr Chandler is."

He tilted his head to the side and his mouth made a small O. "That's impressive. If we can find out who he is, we can work backwards. Please keep me updated."

"I plan to. So, Joy hasn't searched or ordered poison that we know of, she's professing innocence, and based on my observation of her on the day, she was genuinely shocked and upset when he died. I don't think she's that good of an actress. If she'd meant for him to die, she would've at least smirked or had fake tears."

"I agree that her distress wasn't manufactured. But on the other hand, he'd broken up with her, and she was angry at him, and he was chasing money she owed him. And, the obvious, she made the coffee and handed him the cup in front of witnesses. We also found a small container that had the poison in it in the café storeroom with her fingerprints on it. Anna said that container has been there for a while and used to have tea leaves in it. So either Miss Stick repurposed it, or someone else wearing gloves did."

"What about DNA?"

"It's in the queue for testing now."

I sat back and stretched my legs out in front of me, crossing one ankle over the other. "So, do we believe the friend that Joy knew that Alan was coming in?"

He linked his hands and rested them on his belly. "I'll get PC Patel to check over the phone records and social media and this time look for his number or any texts or messages. I can't spare anyone else, so it might take a couple of days, unless you want to help?"

I smiled. "I can spare an hour or so. The quicker we can do this, the quicker I can write another stunning article." I was saying that tongue in cheek—I didn't really think my articles were stunning. The best I could do was factually accurate. But then again, I should give myself more props—I'd won an award. It was still hard to believe. The negative self-talk came from Brad and my family. I needed to remember that and be kinder to myself.

"Excellent. Thanks, Winters. And I'm sure you'll get a detailed, in-depth article out of this. But please run it by me first. I don't want you to give too much of the behind-the-scenes police work away."

"Fair enough. I'll make sure you okay everything before I submit the story." Would it be the story of Joyless's framing and innocence, or would it be a story of unrequited love and revenge? I still wasn't sure.

He gave a nod. "Thank you." He stood. "Okay, let's go out there, and I'll explain to PC Patel what I need, and he can get you started."

I stood. "Sounds like a plan."

CHAPTER 13

My hour at the station turned into two, but I didn't mind—it was fun trying to uncover a clue. Problem was, I found nothing. Patel was still going through the phone records when I left—that girl could talk. I'd done all her social media messages, and boy, was she a massive gossiper. There were quite a few messages about how much she hated me. She also said some nasty things about a few other people in Manesbury. I wrote their names down in case I ever needed support against Joyless.

Whilst I wanted to take photos of some of the messages to show my friends later so they knew how horrible she was, I didn't. It was unethical, and I didn't want to do anything that might get back to Bellamy. Ghosts or no ghosts, he'd revoke my access to evidence and information quicker than I could say possum.

On the way back to the office, I stopped at an ice cream shop and bought a cone with one scoop of chocolate and one of lemon sorbet. It was so good that I decided I might as well do an article on the shop. The manager was happy to answer a few questions, which was great because I needed something to write about today. Hmm, maybe I could do a review on every ice cream store from Manesbury to Exeter. I could even claim the ice creams as expenses.

The ice cream shop was a few miles from Manesbury, and it was a lovely day, not much traffic for a change. The music pumped out of my phone on its holder. I sang along, mostly in tune—the ice cream and this drive were the highlights of my week. I wasn't going to dwell on how sad that was.

A couple of miles out from Manesbury, I looked in my mirror, and a car that hadn't been there a minute ago was right on my tail. *Sheesh, too close, buddy.* It was one lane either way, and the lines were spaced, so if they wanted to drive fast enough to lose control, they could overtake me. Instead, they bumped me from behind.

What the hell?

My heart raced, and I gripped the steering wheel tightly, my breath coming in pants. I couldn't see the driver because of the sun reflecting off the windscreen. Had they done that on purpose? Should I slow down or speed up, pull over? I didn't want to go over the speed limit because they were intimidating me, but they were going to run me off the road if they kept that up.

Again they shunted me. The car lurched forward and to the left a bit. I wrestled with the steering wheel, trying to keep Daisy on the road. If I slammed on the brakes, would it be my fault if there was an accident? Had they already damaged my car? Bloody hell.

They rammed me harder this time, and my wide eyes checked the car in my mirror.

My voice wobbled with adrenaline and fear as I white-knuckled the steering wheel, bracing for another impact. "Hey, Siri, call nine, nine, nine on speaker." I checked my mirror again, and they were still close behind. What was I going to do?

"Calling nine, nine, nine on speaker."

If I pulled over, would they storm the car and do something to me?

There still wasn't anyone coming the other way, so the car whipped out from behind me and accelerated. They were next to me. I swallowed, my pulse throbbing in my ears.

Oh God. What were they doing?

I glanced across, and the driver's shoulders twisted away from me. Instinct told me what he was going to do. As the dispatcher's voice came from my phone, I jammed my teeth together and slammed on my brakes. My tyres screeched. I skidded to a stop as the black car swerved into my lane.

My eyes bugged out. "Oh my God. Oh. My. God."

"Hello. Emergency service operator. Which service do you require? Fire, police, or ambulance?"

My breath sawed in and out in frantic bursts. "Police."

"I'll just connect you now."

"Hello, what is the nature of your emergency?"

"A black BMW sedan has just tried to run me off the road."

I stared at the car as it drove into the distance. There was no number plate on the back. Were they going to turn around for a second try?

"What's your name, phone number, and location?"

I started down the road again. There was nowhere to park, and I'd rather be in a business car park than out here like a sitting duck. A couple of cars drove past, coming the other way, and another car was coming up behind me but at normal speed. I answered the dispatcher and told her I was pulling into a roadside fruit and veg shop.

"Okay. Is anyone injured?"

Other than excessively sweaty palms and a thudding heart, I seemed to be okay. "No."

"We'll have someone there shortly. If that car comes back, call us again."

"Okay, thanks." I hung up and tried to get my breathing under control. Why were people so crazy? I was doing the speed limit, maybe even a couple of miles over. Why wouldn't they just beep at me if they were in that much of a hurry? That driver could've killed me.

Had they meant to?

I stared at the road on full alert, my car still running. Was that random or targeted? *No, don't go there. You're making a big deal out of this.* Well, it *was* kind of a big deal, but not in that way. No one was after me. That was just a crazy person, and I was in the wrong place at the wrong time.

Poor Daisy. I decided it was safe to turn her off, and I got out. I hurried around the back on unsteady legs. My jaw clenched as I anticipated the damage. *Stupid maniac.* Anger clawed through the shock, and my fists clenched. I wanted to punch them in the face. The back of Daisy was dented, chips of black paint embedded into her happy yellow. The bumper bar was twisted as well. This was going to need fixing. And my excess was five hundred pounds because I had no idea who the other driver was. Luckily, I had savings. Still, it was going to hurt, and it wasn't even my fault.

The police arrived within ten minutes, two officers I didn't know, so they weren't from Cramptonbury. I explained what happened, and they took photos of the back of my car. They said they'd put a call-out for other officers to keep a lookout, but that was all they could do since I didn't get a good look at the driver or any number plate.

It made me feel helpless. How dare that person do that and just drive off? And if they did that to me, how many other people were they harassing? Maybe it was a stolen car. Surely someone wouldn't dent and scratch their own car on purpose.

The police made sure I was okay to leave, and they followed me until I got to Manesbury and parked near work. I gave them a wave and went into the office. Carina, Finn, and Zeus were in there. I shut the door, and Zeus pawed my leg, wanting to be picked up.

Carina's smile and magenta hair were as happy and bright as spring flowers. "Hey, Aves. How's your day going?"

Finn gave me a chin tip and went back to his computer. He must be trying to finish something. I put my stuff on my desk, picked Zeus up, and buried my face in his fur. When I'd absorbed enough purrs and fought off impending tears, I looked at Carina. "Someone just tried to run me off the road." It was all I could do to keep my voice steady. Argh, I hated the adrenaline comedown. I might also have a problem with people showing concern for me, but I wasn't going to go there.

She gasped and jumped up. Finn's head jerked up from his work, and he said, "What happened? Are you all right?" Even he got up and came over. They both checked me out from head to toe.

"I'm okay. Still a bit shaken up." I explained what happened.

Finn's tight expression was the kind a man wore before getting into a fight. Carina threw her arms around me and hugged me and the cat. "Oh, Avery. D'at's frightening." She pulled back. "Are you sure you're okay? Do you want a cup of tea?"

I shook my head. "No, that's okay."

"Did you get their number plate details?" Finn asked.

"Nope. They didn't have one on the back. I was looking for it, but there was nothing but black."

"What cases are you working on at the moment?" Finn's

blue eyes pinned me. He expected the truth. This time, I had no trouble giving it to him.

"Just Joyless's. I did go to a story, but we couldn't publish it because the woman was making unfounded complaints. I told Julian I didn't want to run it, and he agreed. But this woman didn't have a black BMW that I know of. I'm also not sure she's the sort of person who would try and run someone off the road." The car parked in her driveway had been a white VW Golf, and even though she was a complainer, she was more likely to call someone about it rather than do something to the person she didn't like.

Finn folded his arms. "Are you sure she's not that kind of person? Do we really know anyone, especially someone you've spent all of ten minutes with?"

"I don't know for sure, but I'll bet you a dinner at the pub that it's not her."

He grinned, his dratted dimples making an appearance. "We might never find out who it is. Trust you to take the low-risk bet."

"Well, I'm not an idiot." I rolled my eyes in mock annoyance. Zeus batted my jaw with a paw. It was so soft. I kissed the top of his head.

Carina gave me a wary look. "Aw, don't go getting so attached, lovie."

"C's right." Finn's sad expression was a hint that he was going to miss the cat too.

"I know. And I'm sorry I made you mind him, and now you love him too."

His chest rose with his fortifying breath. "Yeah, well, I was trying to do a friend a solid."

For a moment, his eyes lost any artifice, and the care and vulnerability I saw there shot straight to my heart. I gave him a sad smile. "I know. Thank you, Vinegar. I really do appreciate it. And so does Zeus." I waved his paw at Finn to break the intense vibe pinging between us because I was probably the only one feeling it. Letting myself get lost in his eyes was likely to end in him backing away faster than Bethany when I asked for my messages. *Play it cool, Avery.*

Carina and Finn smiled at my diversion. Phew. But Finn wasn't quite ready to stop with the emotional stuff, even if he was no longer staring at me as if we were sharing a moment. "We're giving him to Josie today; don't forget."

I cocked my head to the side. "How could I forget?"

Carina's lips curled up on one side. "You did almost get killed today. T"ings like d'at have a way of getting in the way of remembering important t'ings."

I hitched one shoulder up. "Hmm, yeah, I guess. But a little thing like that isn't enough to stop me from remembering. I've been dreading this day for a while." Zeus had enough of my cuddle. He squirmed, and I loosened my arms so he could jump to the floor.

We all worked for the rest of the afternoon, and then I left with Finn. He'd walked Zeus to work, so I gave them a lift home. When we got out, he inspected the back of Daisy. "That's, um…. That happened while you were driving?"

I stared at the scraped, dented metal. "Yep. I'm just so lucky I can read body language. As soon as his shoulder shifted, I knew." I shuddered in a breath and tried to shake off the goosebumps smothering my arms. "If I hadn't, I would've lost control, and God knows where I would've ended up." I'd rather forget about it, so I changed the subject. "Let's go in and get his stuff and take it across."

He gave me an apologetic look. "Okay."

Zeus trotted happily ahead, as far as his lead allowed, oblivious to our sorrow. At least I'd get to see him for the next three weeks. Maybe whoever adopted him would let me come visit? And why was I so attached already? I hadn't even looked after him at my place. Did I need a pet more than I realised? I wasn't lonely, was I? Best not to think too hard on that. I had my friends, and that should be enough.

We gathered everything from Finn's place and walked it across. Josie was waiting for us at the door. "Right on time. And look at that handsome fellow."

Finn gave her a cheeky grin. "Why thank you?"

She slapped him lightly on the upper arm. "Not you, silly boy."

I lifted Zeus and handed him to her. "Meet Zeus. The cutest kitty in Manesbury."

"He fetches, and I've trained him to sit."

My mouth dropped open. "You didn't tell me that!"

"He really only got it properly this morning before work, but when you came in and told me what happened, I forgot."

Josie looked at me with concern. "What happened?"

I gave Finn a "why did you have to tell her that?" look. "It's nothing, really. Just a horrible person on the road today. They almost made me have an accident." It was Finn's turn to give me a "you're hopeless" look. I'd spoken about it enough today, and I didn't want Josie fussing over me. She was doing me enough of a favour by agreeing to take Zeus for three weeks.

"Oh, that's terrible. Anyway, you're all right, yeah?"

I smiled. "Yeah. I'm just so grateful that you're looking after Zeus. I really app—"

Finn pointed at himself and me. "*We* really appreciate it."

"Sorry, *we*."

"I'm sorry I can't take this wee one for longer. He is a cutie." She stroked his back, and he gently pawed her face.

"Let's go inside, and you can show me all his para-phernalia."

Finn and I spent the next hour chatting with Josie, and I made the most of my time, throwing a mouse toy for Zeus to fetch, then giving him cuddles. Josie was fine with me coming by early to take him for a walk and dropping around in the afternoon for a play. As Finn and I walked across the street to go home, his voice was gentle when he said, "Are you sure you want to do all that? You're going to get even more attached."

A despondent sigh heaved out of me. "I'm already super attached. Besides, there's no way I can know he's across the road and not go and visit him. Every time I see Josie's house, I'll think of Zeus being in there. I don't know how you could just cut yourself off like that."

He shrugged. "Maybe it's a man thing? Cut things loose, don't look back."

I side-eyed him. Did I believe him? "Maybe you just don't like dealing with your emotions. Maybe *that's* a man thing?"

"Nope. I'm fine with feeling things. I just refuse to dwell. Moving forward without baggage is how I like to live my life. Dwelling, dragging things out, it never ends well."

"If you say so." Sure, there were instances where that was appropriate, but this wasn't one of them. The love I experienced when I interacted with that cute, energetic ball of fur filled my heart. And while my heart would ache when I lost him, there would be something exquisite about the pain. I would have my memories and the knowledge that he knew he was loved. I just hoped he didn't miss me. Surely once he was with his forever home, he'd settle in and forget about this short time in his life. I couldn't entertain the thought that he might miss me and Finn, too, and now Josie. He was obviously an adaptable cat—all this upheaval in his short life, from breeder to Rosa to Finn to Josie, and he was still the same affectionate, fun-loving cat. I'd reached my gate and Finn his. I gave a half-hearted wave. "See ya."

"Bye, Lightning."

I let myself in with no commentary from Mrs Crabby. Her cantankerous behaviour had been painful from the beginning, but now that she was quiet, I almost missed it. Okay, I didn't miss it, but I found myself worrying about her, and that was worse than being annoyed by her. I knocked. She didn't answer, so I knocked again.

Finally, she came to the door and opened it. Her usually neat hair was sticking up at all angles, she was still in her dressing gown, which had food stains on the front, and she had red eyes, likely from crying. "What do you want?"

"Just checking that you're still alive." I didn't know how she'd take it if I was too nice, so I'd leave it at that rather than admit I was worried about her.

"Why do you care?"

"I'll admit that you're not very nice to me, and we're far from friends, but I know you're going through a hard time, and if we can't show some care to our neighbours, there's something wrong in the world. If I was struggling, I'd want someone to check on me." I didn't say the obvious—there was no one else checking on her. That would be like a kick to the stomach, another reminder that the one person who would've checked was the reason I was at her door.

My candour seemed to have shaken her sour expression loose. "Thank you, Avery. I'm still alive, as you see. No need to panic. Now, if you don't mind, I have things to do." She shut the door before I could say anything else. She wouldn't be Mrs Crabby if she wasn't at least a little rude.

Happy she was still alive—something I never thought I'd say—I continued upstairs. When I got inside, I called to Everly. After hassling her about telling me who killed her, I wasn't sure she'd show, but she did. Phew. "Hey, Everly. I'm not going to pressure you today. I wanted to ask you a question about your mum."

She narrowed her eyes. "It better not be about my murder."

"No. She's struggling, which you already know because I bet you're down there hanging out with her, but I wanted to know if she had a favourite cake or biscuit or food in general. I wanted to make something to take to her."

Her mouth opened slightly in surprise. "Oh. Um...." Should I feel guilty that me doing something kind for her mother was such a shock? Hmm, no. I'd be just as shocked if Mrs Crabby was spontaneously nice to me.

"So?"

"She loves those chocolate-coated marzipan pieces."

I tried not to gag. Marzipan. Argh. There could be no other food and one piece of marzipan left in the world, and she was welcome to it. I shuddered. "Oh, that's easy enough. Thanks."

"You're really going to do something nice for *Mrs Crabby*?"

"Yep. Don't get me wrong, it doesn't mean I like her, but I'm not heartless. She doesn't have anyone. I want her to know she's not forgotten by the whole world."

The scepticism in her eyes dissipated. Her expression softened. "Thank you, Avery. That's kind of you." Her sigh was so soft that I almost missed it. "I know it's her fault. She has a sister and two nieces and a nephew, a couple of cousins. They all used to be close with her, but since my disappearance, she pushed everyone away. She wasn't always that spiky."

I smiled and made air quotes with my fingers. "'Spiky' may be an understatement."

She chuckled. "Yeah. But once upon a time, she was actually nice. Not that she was Disney-princess sweet, but she only showed her teeth when there was something to be legitimately annoyed at. Anyway, thank you for being compassionate."

"It's nothing." I held back on bringing up the whole "maybe you should tell me who killed you and give her closure" thing. It wasn't easy.

My phone rang. Everly said, "That's my cue to leave. See you later."

She disappeared, and I answered my phone. "Sergeant Bellamy. I didn't expect to hear from you again today."

"I have some news about Miss Stick's case, and I heard about your road-rage incident."

"You make it sound like I was road raging." I chuckled. "Anyway, what's the news on the case?" I had no idea how he'd found out since the attending police weren't related to Cramptonbury Station. Maybe Finn had called him, but why?

"Patel found two people we're going to talk to. It could be the breakthrough we've been waiting for."

"Oh, spill the deets." *Oops*. I was becoming a bit too comfortable with our working relationship. "Um, sorry, Sergeant. Can you give me more information?"

At least amusement rather than annoyance coloured his tone. "Patel found text messages between Miss Stick, an ex-friend of hers, and the ex-friend's fiancé. It seems as if Miss Stick had a one-night stand with the fiancé. The ex-friend and fiancé stayed together and ganged up on Miss Stick, blaming her for the entire incident. There was also a phone call between the ex-friend and Miss Stick three days before the murder."

"That sounds promising, but why would you think she'd set her up? I mean, she has motive, but did she threaten Joy in those messages?"

"Nothing specific, but yes. She also made the comment that she 'should be in prison for the pain she inflicts on others.'

She also said, 'I won't rest until you've paid for what you did to me.'"

"Wow, textbook clichés. She could be a movie villain. When are you going to interrogate her?"

He coughed. "Interrogate is too strong a word. We're going to have a chat to her first, look at her bank records, internet history, et cetera. We've managed to fast-track a warrant. Then we'll see about interrogating her. I'll keep you posted."

"Okay, great. Good luck." I was getting ready to hang up, but he wasn't done yet, which was what I was afraid of.

"Finn told me about the car incident. I don't like that you're shrugging it off. I spoke to one of the officers who attended the scene." I should've known he could just look that stuff up. Blech. "It sounds like more than a random incident. There were no other complaints about that car this afternoon. Funny how they were just enraged with you."

I swallowed, the beginnings of anger uncoiling in my gut. "Are you insinuating that I was driving badly or did something to them first?"

His voice was that of a patient father explaining something to a child. "No, Winters, of course not. I'm suggesting that there's more to it and that you should be vigilant from now on."

"But no one, other than Joy, hates me. I haven't pinged off any criminals lately." Or had I?

"Are you su—"

Crash.

I jerked my head around. The living-room window smashed, shards spearing everywhere as a dark object landed with a thud on the floor. I gasped, and trying to avoid the glass on the ground, ran to the window to see if I could see who'd thrown it.

"Winters, what was that? Are you all right? Did I just hear breaking glass?"

I stared out the shattered window to the shadowed night, one of the timber dividers hanging straight down in the middle, barely holding on. "Yes, I'm okay. Someone threw something through my window. I'll let you know what in a minute. I saw a dark figure just before they ran into the laneway where I park my car, but they're gone." I licked my lips, eager to give chase, but it was too late. By the time I got downstairs, they'd have driven off—I had to assume there was a getaway car waiting for them.

"I'll send someone down. Sit tight."

I had one last stare into the gloom. Other than a dog that started barking at the noise, all was quiet. I spun around and spied the projectile. "It's a brick." I frowned. "I think there's paper stuck to it."

"Don't touch anything. We'll sort it when we come down."

"Yes, Sergeant." The note was affixed sturdily with a thick rubber band. The large writing in black marker couldn't have been clearer. At least I wasn't going to be in suspense waiting for the police. "It says 'Back off, Avery Winters,' and there's a skull and crossbones as well."

"You didn't touch it, did you?"

"No. You can't miss the note. They weren't subtle." With either the delivery or the message.

"Do you still think the car incident was random?" His breathing increased, as if he was walking.

"Hmm, I'm still thinking about it." If I admitted it was targeted, I would have to allow people to tell me to stay home and be careful. Not that I wasn't going to be careful, but I had a life to live. If I stayed home every time someone was out to get me, I'd never leave.

"As I said, sit tight, and we'll be there soon. Call me if anything else happens between now and then."

"Yes, Sergeant. Bye."

He hung up, and I stared forlornly at the mess. After the police checked it out, I'd have to clean this up. Lucky Zeus wasn't here. He could've been hurt. Imagine if he'd been sitting where the brick landed. He would've been killed.

There was a knock on my door. My heart thudded heavily. *No, don't be stupid. As if they'd knock. They'd probably force their way in when you were asleep.* Maybe.

I looked through the peephole. Mrs Crabby. I opened the door. "Hello, Mrs Collins."

She scowled. "What was that noise? Did you break something?"

I would've shut my eyes for thinking time, but I wasn't about to lose a visual of the woman. She was liable to do anything. "No. I didn't." Now I'd have to admit someone else vandalised her house, and she was going to kick me out. She'd made it clear that I'd brought enough disharmony to her home. To be fair, she'd been injured by one of the degenerates who'd tried to kill me. On the bright side, maybe this was my chance to move and adopt Zeus. "I'm sorry, but someone threw a brick through the window. I'm waiting for the police to show up. Once they're gone, I'll clean up the mess. I'll arrange to have the window fixed at my own cost." It wasn't her fault this happened, and even if she had insurance, there'd be an excess to pay. I'd at least do the right thing.

Being targeted was getting expensive.

She stared at me for a moment, probably processing everything. The weird look she gave me was indecipherable. "Good. You can contact the agent, and they'll give you numbers for the preferred repairers. Please make sure it's done tomorrow."

Wow, no massive lecture. That was a first. "Okay. Thank you. And sorry for the noise."

She lifted her chin and regarded me. Her chin dropped in a stern nod. Then she turned and went back downstairs. What just happened? How did I not get kicked out? Maybe me being nice to her had come at the right time, or maybe she had no energy to get angry enough to tell me to leave. Whatever the reason, I was thanking my guardian angel.

The police arrived seven minutes later. Bellamy was there with a middle-aged, short-haired, plain-clothes detective I'd never met before. "Miss Winters, this is Detective Sergeant Pierce Rogers. He works with a group of stations in our council area, and he's kindly agreed to come here tonight."

He held out his hand. "Pleasure to meet you, Miss Winters."

I shook it. "Likewise, Detective Sergeant. I'm sorry for the bother."

He brushed his fingers across his thick moustache. "Catching criminals is not a bother—it's my job. Now, can we see the evidence?"

I stepped aside, and they came in. I pointed to the brick. "Just be careful of the glass." That was an obvious thing to say, but I felt like I had to say something. *Awkward.*

The detective Sergeant peered out the window, then took a photo of the living room and mess. Bellamy put gloves on and picked up the brick. They both looked at it, and then the detective sergeant asked me to go through what happened. Even though Bellamy had been there at the time, I went through it all. Then he asked me about the car incident. When we finished, he nodded. "Okay. Thank you for your cooperation, Miss Winters. I'm sure Sergeant Bellamy has already said this, but you need to be careful until the case with Miss Stick is fully investigated. She asked you to help get her out, did she not?"

"Yes. She did." I wasn't sure where this was going.

"Well, Sergeant Bellamy and I have a suspicion that she didn't commit the crime, and someone is trying to stop you uncovering what really happened. It's just a suspicion, mind you, but we think it's best if you curtail any outings for the next few days."

Outings? He thought going to work was an outing? "I have to do my job. There's no way I can sit here all day and do nothing."

Bellamy stepped in. "Can you interview people via the phone?"

I blew out a huge breath. "Yes, I suppose so, but it's not the same. I also can't get the pictures I want if I do that. Besides, they obviously know where I live, so what's to stop them coming here again but with something more deadly, like a Molotov cocktail? Or they could bash the doors in and knife me." Hmm, a little dramatic, but I wanted to get my point across. If someone wanted me dead, a couple of locked doors weren't going to stop them.

Bellamy gave me a stern look. "That's true; however, we want them to think you're taking them seriously, that you're scared. If they see that and think you're going to give up chasing answers, they'll leave you alone at least long enough for us to find out who's behind this."

He couldn't promise that. No one could.

After my stress-filled day, I had no spoons left to argue. I'd just agree with them and formulate a plan tomorrow. "Okay, Sergeant. I'll stay home tomorrow and see how I go."

He was visibly relieved. "Thank you, Miss Winters. I appreciate it. I would hate for something to happen to you."

I'd heard that before, and whilst I believed it, if something did happen to me, he would get over it pretty quickly.

The detective sergeant turned to Bellamy. "Right. We've got some policing to do. Let's see if we can get some answers."

"Righto." Bellamy peered at me. "Are you fine to be here by yourself? I can't spare anyone to watch the place, but I could ask Finn to come over."

That would be worse than the brick coming through the window. Me and Finn alone at night while I was exhausted and emotional, I was liable to throw myself at him. Not a great idea. "Ah, no thanks. If I'm worried, I can call Meg."

"As you wish. Good night, Miss Winters."

"Good night, Sergeant Bellamy, Detective Sergeant."

They left, and I cleaned up the mess. All the while, slow-burning anger simmered deep inside, gathering heat.

The warning couldn't have been clearer: *Back off, Avery Winters.*

My response? Not a chance.

CHAPTER 14

Before going to bed last night, I called Charles. He came and hung out in the living room, ready to warn me if he heard anything. He left when I got up, bleary-eyed and exhausted. It had taken me an age to fall asleep as I ran all the facts of Joyless's case over and over again, trying to see what I'd missed. There was only one conclusion I could come to, and I felt simultaneously like an idiot that it had taken me so long but also stupid for thinking I was a worry to Mr Chandler. Because it couldn't be anyone else. Ironfist must have told him about my visit to the police station. Mr Chandler could obviously speak to ghosts. Even if there was a middle-person involved in the relaying of messages, it was clear that Chandler was communicating with the ghost. Had Ironfist overheard other things before I'd gone there? He must know that we were trying to find out who his boss was. I didn't have confirmation about this, but there was nothing else that made sense. Not to mention that Ironfist had threatened me.

The only thing I couldn't work out was, why go after me?

We didn't have anything on Mr Chandler, and by doing this, he was risking leaving more clues as to who he was.

Unless we were closer to discovering his identity than we thought?

Hmm….

At eight, I went across the road and took Zeus for a short walk. I didn't want to go too far from home after Bellamy's warning, but it was more about not putting Zeus in danger. When I returned, I had a cup of tea with Josie. She looked across her round table at me. "I'm not sure you know, but what's up with Marge? I haven't seen her around the last few days. She normally wanders up to the village once a day."

I wasn't sure how much Josie knew about her neighbour, but I'd assume she knew something as she'd lived here for a long time. "I found a locket on my walk the other day, and I put it in the *Manesbury Daily* to see if we could find the owner."

Her brows rose. "Ah, yes! I remember seeing that. Pretty locket."

"Well, turns out it belongs to Everly, Mrs Collins's daughter." I peered at Josie, waiting for her facial expression to give away whether she knew or not.

Her mouth made an O. "Her missing daughter?"

"Yes." The ghost who haunts my apartment. If only I could add that.

"Oh." She frowned. "Ooooh. No wonder she hasn't been out. Have you checked on her?"

I warmed my hands on the mug. "Yes. Last time was after I saw you yesterday, and then last night, someone threw a brick through my window, and she came to check what happened."

"That was my next question. I heard a commotion last night, and when I looked out the window, I didn't see anything." They really needed better street lighting in our little dead-end. "Why would someone do that?"

"Probably stupid teenage vandals. Who knows?" I wasn't about to worry her. "Which reminds me. I have to call the agent this morning and get numbers for window people." Hmm, glaziers. That was the word I'd been looking for. Oh well.

I finished my tea, gave Zeus one last cuddle, and returned to the scene of the crime. I didn't bother knocking on Mrs Crabby's door. I'd see her later to confirm when the window was fixed.

After ringing the agent, I called two of the glaziers. One could come ASAP, so I booked them. Then I called Julian and told him I'd be working from home, but I didn't elaborate as to why. He was fine with it, which I was coming to know was his way. He was the best boss ever. As long as we got the work done, he didn't care if we did it from the moon.

After all the boring stuff was out of the way, I called Bellamy. "Winters. Is everything okay?"

"Yes, it's fine. They're coming to fix the window soon. I just wanted to get the name of Joy's ex-friend and her boyfriend so I can look them up on social media."

"You don't have to do that. We're interviewing them this morning."

I rolled my eyes. Why could he never just go with what I was asking? "I know, but I've been targeted for a reason, and I want to do what I do best and research. Maybe I won't find anything, but we're missing a detail. I know we are." My sixth sense always kicked in at some point during research for an article and lately in murder investigations. I didn't have the full story, but I should have it if the threats aimed at me were any hint. "Otherwise, why target me? I must've come across something and not realised it. Besides, there's not much else I can do from home except get on the internet and look at stuff... you know, because I'm not allowed to leave my flat." Okay, so I hadn't followed that super strictly, but if I went into the village or the office, he'd be sure to hear about it, and then I'd hear about it. I hoped he would feel the tiniest bit of sympathy and relent, if only to keep me quiet.

He huffed. "Fine. Hang on a moment." After a minute, he came back on. "Elanor Black and Oscar Klein. They're both twenty-five years old. Both Caucasian with brown hair—just in case you have trouble finding them, a description might help."

"Okay, great. Thanks, Sergeant. I appreciate it." The buzzer for the security door rang. "I have to go. I think the window people are here. I'll let you know if I find anything."

"Same here. Take care." He hung up. No goodbye for me.

I poked my head out of the broken pane, careful not to cut myself on the remaining glass shards. Yep, it was the window people. I went to the intercom and pressed the button to let them in. While they got to work, I sat at the kitchen table and opened my laptop.

I started with Facebook. I found Elanor, but Oscar didn't seem to be on it. Thankfully, her stuff wasn't set to private. Her latest posts included photos of Oscar… at least I thought it was him. Photos of their engagement party. Of a recent holiday to Spain. A barbecue at a friend's. I scrolled back a couple of years. No photos of her with Joyless. She must've deleted them all. That's how much she hated her. I didn't blame her. There were photos of her with the two women who were at the station yesterday. So she didn't have a falling out with the whole group.

Next, I hopped onto Instagram. Both she and Oscar had accounts there. His posts were sporadic and nothing much to write home about. Her stuff was the same as Facebook, with a few extra bikini shots. Hmm… what was this one from a year and a half ago? I peered at the screen and enlarged it.

Oscar wasn't in the picture, but Elanor stood there with a

woman I didn't recognise and Camilla, their arms around each other. It was the banner behind them, and the person Camilla had her arm around on her other side that had my mouth dropping open.

Happy Engagement, Camilla and Alan.

Alan's grin was as large as Camilla's, and his hand gripped her waist tightly. They'd been engaged, and now they weren't together. And what had come after their engagement? Alan dating Joyless. What in Hades had happened there, and why was Camilla still friends with Joyless? Had Camilla broken up with Alan and given them the okay to date? I needed to talk to Alan. I didn't want to invite him here, but I couldn't go somewhere Bellamy might hear about.

This was too big a deal not to follow up. I eyed the two window-repair guys. They weren't even halfway done. They'd likely be here for another forty-five minutes to an hour. This had to wait, which annoyed me because I wanted to know now.

Instead of stressing, I ordered some chocolate-covered marzipan online, then looked up Camilla's Instagram—she'd liked a few of Elanor's posts, so it was easy to follow her back to her account. There were no pictures of her and Alan. The evidence had been scrubbed away.

So, she wasn't as blasé about it as I'd thought. Although, what was the point of having photos of an ex-fiancé on your page, especially since you were now with someone else?

This line of thought wasn't necessarily going to lead us to who killed Alan, but it was worth pursuing. As soon as the glaziers left, I sat on the couch and pictured Alan. "Alan Albertson, please come here. I'm inviting you into my home." Nothing happened. Had he already transitioned? I repeated myself. I felt like I should have a Ouija board in front of me and television cameras recording a fake moment meant to sell someone's talking-to-the-dead services. How many of them were real? I used to think they were all dodgy, but, well, I knew differently now. Probably most were still frauds. That made me realise that if I didn't care what the wider world thought of me, I could probably do this for a living—help people talk to their dead relatives. Somehow that felt wrong. Not that it was, but I wasn't desperate, and I had a job I loved. It would also ensure that I lost Finn as a friend. Not only would he never speak to me again, he'd hate me forever.

Alan appeared. "Avery?" He looked slightly confused and glanced around. "Where am I?"

I smiled. "You're at my flat. I invited you here because I need to ask about something."

"Oh." He ran a hand through his hair and rested the other hand on his hip. "Okay, then. Ask away."

"Oops, hang on." I went to the dining table and grabbed my pen and notebook. There was no point trying to record him with my phone since I was the only one who could hear him, so I'd have to write it all down. I sat back on the couch. "Right. You used to be engaged." He stared at me, his eyebrows raised, clearly surprised at this line of questioning. "What happened between you and Camilla, and what did Joy have to do with it?"

"How did you know about that? Did Joy tell you?"

"No. I discovered it for myself, but I'm going to speak to Joy and Camilla separately after this, so your story better match theirs." Being rude probably wasn't the best way to go about this because he could refuse to talk to me about it. I wanted the truth, not his sanitised version that made him look better. "What happened? Who broke it off and why?" He folded his arms and turned his back to me. "I'm not trying to put you on the spot to judge you, and I'm sorry if I'm asking you to regurgitate a painful part of your life, but it might be important. Not only should you want me to get to the bottom of who killed y——"

He spun around, red blotches on his cheeks. Whilst he wasn't shouting, his volume left no doubt that he was unhappy. "We know who killed me! Joy did it. She handed me the goddamned cup, for God's sake." His eyes widened. "She is in jail still, isn't she?"

I deserved a medal for not rolling my eyes. "Yes, she's still in jail. But what if she didn't do it? Should she still be in jail? Picture this——her boyfriend broke up with her, and then she was framed for killing him. Is that fair?"

"Is it fair that I broke up with her, and she lied to everyone about who broke up with whom? Is it fair that she threw herself at me time and time again while I was engaged and when I finally couldn't take it any more, cheated, and then she told Camilla it was all me? That's why Camilla broke up with me. Doesn't that tell you all you need to know about Joy's character? Oh, and don't forget the money she refused to pay back."

Right, so now we were getting to the bottom of it. Where was his culpability in all this? "Let's pretend that you know you did the wrong thing by cheating and that Joy didn't control your thoughts and actions. Last I checked, you had free will." He gave me a dirty look but said nothing, thank God. I didn't want to spend my time with him arguing. I just wanted answers. "Anyway… what happened after that? Camilla is friends with Joy. How and when did that come about? And did you have any contact with Camilla after it all went down?"

"You really think Joy didn't kill me?"

I ditched any judgement from my eyes and replaced it with genuine care. "I don't think so. I don't know for sure, but I need to know. She's not my favourite person, so I have no problem with her being incarcerated for a long time… but only if she's guilty. And there's enough of a doubt that our conversation is important." I had the brief thought that I was a sucker, that I was still letting people walk all over me—Mrs Crabby, Joy—by giving them the benefit of the doubt and trying to be kind when they needed me to be.

He stared at the floor for a bit, then raised his head slowly to look at me. "I'm not proud of what happened. After Camilla broke up with me, I knew she would never forgive me, so I apologised to her and her family, but that was it. I didn't try and work things out with her. It also made me realise that we weren't ready for marriage. If I'd truly loved her, I wouldn't have failed her so badly. Other than the guilt, it was easier to continue things with Joy. I never once thought we'd be it for each other, but it was fun for a while." His gaze moved to the couch. "Is it okay if I sit?"

I almost laughed but kept myself in check. "Of course." Ghosts didn't get tired and didn't need to sit. Maybe it was a force of habit.

He settled on the other end of the couch. "Joy crawled back to Camilla after I broke things off with her, and the last few months of my life, Camilla and I were back to being acquaintances. She was in a good place." He gave a stunted laugh. "She even called me a few days before I died to see how I was going, and we spoke about Joy owing me money. She said she'd try and help me get it back. She was the one who suggested I turn up to the coffee shop and give it one last try."

"What?! Didn't you think that was weird? I mean, why would she care?" Smoking gun, anyone?

He blinked and stared at the far wall. "She was having trouble with Joy again. She wanted to talk about it because she knew I'd understand. I think Joy was going after her boyfriend. She was asking me about how she got her claws into me." He rubbed his forehead. "It was awkward, going over it again with her, but it made me see how stupid I'd been. I'd thrown away a good thing for a person that wasn't worth it." He rubbed his chest. "The last couple of months with Joy were torture. She was demanding, irrational, possessive, and she screams and breaks things when she's angry." He shook his head. "Two of my neighbours actually came and saw me one morning after a fight, making sure I was okay." He sighed. "Anyway, when Camilla called me out of the blue a few weeks ago, I didn't want to deny her anything. If she wanted to chat occasionally, I'd be up for it. And when she asked about how Joy got her claws into me, I figured after what I'd done, it was only fair I try and help… atone for my mistakes. And to answer your question: Camilla was upset that Joy owed me money, so she was trying to help by suggesting I go see her."

My eyes widened. "Wow. That's a lot." I cocked my head to the side, not sure if I wanted to comment on the fact that Camilla knew he was going to the café or about how violent Joy was. I went for the easier option. "And doesn't that tell you something? Joy's anger is immediate, and then she cools off. So if she was going to kill you, wouldn't it be in the heat of the moment? Do you think she has the patience to premeditate it and wait for her chance?" Maybe she did, but I needed his opinion on this. I didn't know her well enough.

"She's a grudge holder, but after the moment, her anger subsides. She might put you on her shit list, but she wouldn't stay volcano-style angry." He rubbed his thigh. "Come to think of it, she wouldn't kill me to avoid paying me the money— she'd just lie her way out of it. She did that a lot with her friends. She's a gaslighter." I wasn't going to go into it, but I could relate to that. She'd lied about me to other people, and it wasn't a small lie.

"Are you sure she wouldn't kill you over money? How much was it?"

"Four thousand pounds. She'd talk her parents or some other sucker into giving it to me if I served her with a court order. I can't see her killing me over it, but, of course, never say never."

"What did she use the money for?" This wasn't a necessary question. I was just curious.

"Getting her teeth fixed and Botox. She had veneers put on her front teeth, and forehead injections."

"Right, so every time she looks in the mirror, it's going to remind her of you and that she killed you. Would you really do that to yourself?" I was talking to myself more than Alan, but he answered anyway.

"I wouldn't."

I wrote some notes, then peered at him. "And what about Camilla? Does she seem the sort who would bide her time till an opportunity arose and she could frame someone she hated? Is she even smart enough to do that?" Camilla had seemed a bit daft at the police station, so I didn't know if I was on the right path, but she sure had motive to off both of them. And it looked as if she'd set the whole thing up. "She knew when you were going to the café, yeah, seeing as how she'd suggested it?"

He tapped his thigh while he thought. Realisation seemed to dawn in his eyes. "Ah, yeah, she did, and she's not daft at all. She's competitive and has a law degree, except she doesn't practice." My brows rose. "Her parents are extremely wealthy, and she and her mother run a couple of charities. There's no way she'd get her hands dirty killing someone, even an ex who cheated on her. She's with someone else now, anyway. She'd never do anything to shame her family." He was totally in denial.

I wrote it all down. I added "good actor" into the mix. She'd had me fooled with her I'm-a-ditz act at the station yesterday. "Interesting. So her family is high profile?" The longer this conversation went on, the more I thought I knew who did it. It was so obvious that I'd be an idiot not to notice.

"Her father owns a top-notch law firm in London. Her brother works there, and she and her mother organise charity events and make sure they're seen about town, if you know what I mean."

"Why is she friends with Joy? Why would she hang out around Manesbury?" I imagined that the super-rich preferred to hobnob around London or Surry. Manesbury wouldn't even feature in their vocabulary.

"They play polo and ride regularly. Their farm is here— Camilla's mum grew up in the house they live in now. Camilla and her brother went to a private high school in Exeter. Their dad stayed in London through the week at one of their properties and came home on the weekends. Joy went to the same school—her dad is the principal. He pulled a few strings, and from what Joy told me, they sacrificed so she could go there. That's where they met."

"Okay. They've known each other since how old?"

He shrugged. "I don't know. Probably since they were about fourteen or so. I'm pretty sure they did a few years of school together. I once saw a picture of them at a school camp from year nine."

I didn't bother explaining myself, but basically, they'd been friends for a long time, so Joy's betrayal would've hit hard, especially for someone who was loyal to her family. I was going to assume, for the purposes of this exercise, that loyalty was one of Camilla's traits, and that she would never have betrayed Joy the way she betrayed her. Was that enough for her to frame her and murder someone else? I still couldn't work out how she could target Alan, though. I would've remembered seeing her on my way to the café that morning, and she definitely wasn't inside. The police searched the storeroom and back prep area after it happened. Unless she snuck out the back door? But I would've seen her run through the café at least. Joy would've told Bellamy it was her as well. Joy wouldn't take the rap for someone else. Not in a million years. And definitely not someone whose fiancé she was happy to mess around with.

I could put some pieces together, but I was missing that one link. If Joy wasn't guilty, how did the real killer do it? Were we clutching at straws because of a ghost who might've been toying with me? But why would he do that? I resisted the urge to sigh.

"Has Joy ever stolen any of her other friends' partners?"

"I don't know. I've seen her flirt with one of her sister's boyfriends before. We had a fight about it afterwards. She said she wasn't doing anything, but I saw how she was laughing at all his jokes, and she rubbed his arm a couple of times, did that hair-flip thing. Her sister was glaring at her, but that didn't stop her." He shook his head as if to get the image out of it. "Is that all?"

I had a think. I could've asked Bellamy this later, but I wanted to know now. "What's Camilla's last name?" Her Instagram handle was @Camillaxo, so I had no idea what her surname was, and now Alan was here, I wasn't going to bother trying to find her on Facebook.

"Reuben."

I was disappointed that her surname wasn't Chandler. It would've made this so much easier. Even though Ironfist had called his boss Mr Chandler, he could've been trying to throw me off, or it could've been Camilla's father. He wouldn't be the first parent to step in and fix things for their children. "Okay, great. That's it for now. If I think of something later, can I call you again?"

He looked at me. "I'd prefer if you didn't, but okay." He stood.

"Thanks for the chat."

"Bye, Avery."

"Bye, Alan." He disappeared, and I was left sitting with my notebook, pondering our discussion. Was I onto something? There were so many red flags marking the way to Camilla. I'd have to run it by Bellamy and see if he saw what I saw. You'd have to be an idiot not to, and he wasn't that.

I googled "Camilla Reuben," and details of her father's law firm came up. There were also a couple of articles about her and her family at different events. Hmm, she and her brother were successful polo players. They'd both won their fair share of tournaments. Other than the superficial stuff, there was nothing except work things about her father, which made sense. If you were a high-profile solicitor, you wouldn't want everyone knowing your private business, especially since one facet of his large firm dealt with court cases. Criminals weren't known for their forgiveness, and I was sure more than one hit had been arranged from prison.

I called Bellamy. "Hey, Sergeant."

"Hello, Winters. What's up?"

"I'm not sure if I'm on the right track, but I've found someone who might've killed Alan and framed Joy. But I don't know exactly how they got the poison where it needed to be at the right time."

"We're still looking into one of those other suspects we talked about yesterday. As far as I know, nothing else has happened to give us another suspect."

"I just spoke with Alan."

"You spoke with the victim again? Why?"

"Well, I dug into Elanor's social media, and I noticed

something strange. Camilla, one of Joy's friends who was in your office yesterday—"

"Yes, I know who you're talking about."

"Right, well, she was engaged to Alan. And about a year and a half ago, Joy seduced him—according to Alan—and Camilla found out and broke up with him. He then continued his relationship with Joy until he broke up with her." I hoped I'd get some kind of enthusiasm and not be shot down because he thought it was a stupid direction to go in.

"I see." And that was all I got. Was he considering it?

After a minute of waiting, I lost my patience. "Well? What do you think?"

"Sorry. I'm just googling her. Camilla Reuben. She's from a very wealthy and influential family."

I knew what he wasn't saying. "And we'd better be sure before we go investigating her unless we have some kind of concrete proof?"

"Yes. That's exactly it. She didn't seem too bright when she was here yesterday. How would she mastermind something like that? Not to mention, she wasn't at the crime scene. Did you see her anywhere?"

"No, and that's what I can't work out—how the killer managed to get the poison into the right cup at the right time. But anyway, get this, she has a law degree, and yesterday was an act."

He must've been taking that in because he was quiet for a while. "A law degree? But it doesn't say anywhere that she's a solicitor."

"She's not. She got her degree, and now she runs a couple of charities with her mother."

"Well, she sounds like an upstanding citizen. Does Alan think she did it?"

"He wasn't sure. He said it's possible. But—and here's the

clincher—she knew what day and time he was going to the café." I probably shouldn't push because if he investigated her and she was innocent, he could cop a lot of flak from his superiors and the media. On the surface, she was a model citizen, and she was gorgeous. She'd elicit a lot of sympathy if the police made her look bad and she ended up being innocent. But there were so many reasons to look into her. "Surely there's a discreet way we can do this?" Before I called, I should've considered her father was a solicitor, but in my haste to follow up, I hadn't thought it through. "Also, why did she play dumb yesterday? The stuff she was saying basically cemented that Joy was guilty, or at least it would encourage someone to think so. The way she said it made her look silly rather than calculated."

He cleared his throat. "Possibly." He went silent again. I slumped into the couch. This was about her father being a top solicitor and rich guy. I could just imagine the friends in high places he had.

My voice was gentle. "I know we can't move on this without planning how to do it and be subtle, but after everything Alan told me… she has way more motive than Elanor. And if we look at the framing-Joy angle, it's even more compelling.

"I don't like this, Winters. We're chopping and changing on the say-so of a ghost. For God's sake, am I going to risk my career on your word? And they're friends. Why would she frame her friend? She's clearly made peace with what happened." His tone lowered, and I had to strain to hear it. "It's one thing to accept that you can talk to ghosts, but would I stake my career on it? I just don't know, Winters. Try and get something more concrete, something physical, then come back to me. I have to go. Bye."

Conversation over.

The more I thought about it, the more she looked guilty. And I knew it wasn't because we'd started down this path that I wanted to be right. I didn't like Joy. I couldn't care if she spent a few years in jail… okay, it would probably be more like twenty, but my gut told me she didn't do it. And Ironfist was too arrogant to worry about revealing that someone called Mr Chandler had been involved. At the café, he threw in that Joy did it as an afterthought. He didn't seem that worried that I didn't believe him.

So, how did I find proof that Camilla did it? I needed to find a connection between her and Chandler. But how in Hades was I going to do that?

CHAPTER 15

Google was my friend. My very best friend. I sat at the kitchen table and started laughing. How could it be this easy? It was ridiculous, really. Although, if I hadn't been able to talk to ghosts, none of this would've come to light, so it made sense that Camilla or her father had employed Chandler to take care of it. The article that led me to that conclusion had come up on the first page of my search: *Reuben Solicitors Mr Chandler*.

Innocent! Ethan Robert Chandler Found Innocent in Organised Crime Case. Michael Howey from Reuben Solicitors has successfully defended his client, Ethan Robert Chandler, in a case he says "…has cost my client his exemplary reputation. He is relieved this case is finally over so he can get back to being a productive and valued member of society. My client is considering suing for defamation and libel. News outlets have questioned my client's integrity without proof. Today, my client has been vindicated by the highest court in the land. We have said all along that Mr Chandler is innocent of all charges, and today, the court has agreed."

Would there be any proof of a connection other than that if Bellamy got a court order to search their records? What if the crime boss hadn't paid in full and had left some money owing to be paid back in favours? I would assume some money had been paid to leave a legit paper trail. I didn't expect that everything was above board, though, because engaging someone to kill someone else whilst framing another wasn't a normal reaction to a cheating scandal. The fact they'd done that said to me that there were likely other dodgy things they did.

I probed further.

They had successfully defended, and sometimes not so successfully, other criminals with ties to organised crime. Yes, everyone deserved representation, but Reuben Solicitors seemed to defend more than their fair share of big-time crims. Their ethics were questionable.

The only way there would be evidence would be if they thought they had no chance of being suspected, let alone caught—which would've been the case if it weren't for the ghosts. Unfortunately, we needed evidence that would stand up in court, and I'd have to find it.

I'd start with the weakest link. Definitely Camilla. She was a liar but not a seasoned criminal. Hmm…. Had it been her dad's idea, or had she asked him for help? The other option was that her dad had recorded her phone calls and knew when Alan was going to the shop. Maybe Camilla was unaware of the whole plot? Argh! There were too many choices. If I was sure Camilla had instigated it all, I could try and get a confession out of her. But what if she didn't know about any of it? Would she feel guilty enough to question her father whilst wearing a wire?

I rested my forehead on the table and groaned. Why couldn't things be straightforward?

I lifted my head and sat up straight. This was like a tangle of fishing line. I'd have to carefully unravel it before I could catch the big fish. Letting the different options overwhelm me wasn't going to help. I took a deep breath and fortified myself. I could do this. And I could do it without alerting Camilla or her father that we were onto them.

Unfortunately, I was going to need Joyless's assistance, and she'd know I was trying to help her. Before I did anything, I wanted to speak to Charles.

"Charles, can you come to my place?"

He appeared. "Hey. What's up?"

"Where have you been, just out of interest?"

"Visiting with Everly at the place she does counselling with other ghosts. She's been a bit sad lately."

Guilt froze my tongue for a moment. I felt bad for accidentally finding her locket, but was it a fluke? Out of all the people and after all those years, I was the one to find it? The one who could speak to her ghost, and the one who worked for the paper and could put it in there…. It must be for a reason. The whole thing wasn't really my fault, but pushing her to reveal her killer *was* my fault. If only she would explain why she didn't want anyone to know.

"Avery, what's wrong?"

I shook my head quickly. "It's about the locket and her murder. I've upset her, and I didn't mean to, but I want justice for her. I want her mother to have peace, you know?"

His gaze dropped to his feet. He spoke to them rather than look at me. "I have the opposite problem—no one cared when I died, and my dad was the reason." His eyes finally met mine. "Well, I think my mum cried a bit, but Dad threatened her that if she cried over me, he'd beat her. He did it anyway." His sigh squeezed out from under the weight of a thousand boulders. "Sorry. I didn't mean to make this about me."

"You didn't. Why can't everyone just be nice to each other?" My parents also came to mind. *Argh.*

He gave me a wry grin. "Then Sergeant Bellamy would be out of a job."

I returned his smile. "Well, yeah, and I'd probably be too. Good-news stories don't get the same response as something shocking. Anyway, I was wondering if you've heard anything from your undercover guys?"

"No. I'm hoping they'll come back with something soon. They need time to build trust."

I pressed my lips together. Did we have time? I had no idea how quickly the court system ticked over in England. I crossed my fingers that I had time to figure this out. I told Charles everything I'd learned and what my new hypothesis was. "What do you think? I'm going to see if Joy wants to help us get a confession out of Camilla, but what if Camilla knows nothing about it?"

"Or what if she refuses to come clean?"

"Exactly. I need something that's going to lead to physical evidence. If we could just figure out how they got the poison into the cup."

Charles wriggled his closed lips from side to side as he thought about it. His mouth popped open. "Ironfist was there, right?"

"Yes...." My heart raced. I knew what he was going to say. How had I missed it?

"*He* did it. He's a poltergeist."

"It makes so much sense. He could've slipped the poison into the almond milk when it sat next to the coffee machine." I licked my bottom lip. "And someone else could've put cyanide in that container the night before." I didn't think he could've transported the cyanide from somewhere else, opened a container, put it in, and screwed it shut—he wasn't that powerful—but it was plausible that he could've carried a tiny vial there from close by and taken it back with him, meaning the cyanide in the storeroom container was just for show. This was also going to confuse the process of charging someone with the crime. How could you explain to a judge that a ghost had put poison in the milk? "That poses a problem."

"What do you mean?"

"Well, an actual person didn't put the poison in the cup, and we can't prove they did. The best we could do is charge them with conspiracy to murder, if we find any proof. The issue is getting the court to believe someone other than Joy could've put the poison in there."

"I think you need to talk to Bellamy. He might have a better idea of how we can overcome this."

"And I need to do it in person. If I can go down there, I'll also be able to talk to him about getting Joy in on this." The more we discussed this, the less hopeful I felt.

"Let me know how it goes, and if I hear from the under-cover ghosts, I'll let you know."

"Thanks, Charles. You're awesome."

"So are you." He grinned. "Bye, Avery."

"See ya." I didn't feel awesome. It didn't matter how much I wracked my brain, I couldn't come up with an answer. I picked up my phone. "Sergeant Bellamy, hi."

"Winters, again? Surely you didn't get any proof that quickly."

"No, but I need to come in and discuss something with you. I know how we might be able to get some proof. Would a confession get a conviction?"

"Possibly. We still need to prove beyond reasonable doubt that someone did something."

"And it works the other way, right? If there is reasonable doubt as to whether Joy knew there was poison in that cup, they can't convict her?"

"Yes, but I don't see how anyone can prove that right now."

"Please can I come down and talk to you? As long as this case goes unprosecuted, they'll be after me. I can't stay locked up forever."

He huffed. "I don't have time to come get you."

"It's fine. I can't see them running me off the road twice."

"Can you take the bus?"

I shuddered. I hated public transport because it was full of strangers, and some of them smelled. But if it made him feel better, I'd do it. I'd like to see them try and run a huge, heavy bus off the road. "Okay, I'll take the bus. I'm leaving now. Bye, Sergeant."

"Be careful." He hung up.

I checked the bus timetable, dressed warmly, and grabbed my bag and umbrella—the weather wasn't the best today. There was a bus in five minutes—just enough time to get to the bus stop.

As I hurried down the laneway to the main street through town, I kept watch for any unusual people or cars. Now wasn't the time to think back to the drive-by shooting at A Snip in Time. What if they were done warning me, and they had guns? With each step, I was primed to dive to the ground. My hapkido cat rolls would come in handy.

I felt like a bit of an idiot when I boarded the bus sans incident. They'd only wanted to warn me, and by they, were they connected to Camilla or her dad? I stared out the window as the bus rumbled along. I really had no proof, except circumstantial, that Camilla and/or her dad were behind this. Letting the idea run away from me wasn't ideal, but it seemed to happen with each case. Look in one direction until that was a bust, then go down a new path. I hoped my focus didn't mean I had blinkers on and missed something else.

Had they committed the perfect crime?

Humans weren't perfect. There must be some DNA, a hair dropped, something. A video of someone sneaking in the night before? Anything to cast doubt on Joyless's involvement.

I walked into the station, and my stress must've shown on my face because PC Adams buzzed me in after a quick hello. There wasn't even any ribbing about the tart. When I got to Bellamy's door, it was open, and who should I see sitting opposite him but Ironfist.

I stepped into the room. "Hello, Sergeant." I firmly closed the door behind me and rounded on Ironfist. "I know you're behind that brick through my window. I'm not scared of you or Chandler's thugs. He must be scared to threaten me like that, huh? Worried I've worked it out, and I'm going to take them down one by one? Hmm?" I narrowed my eyes and glared like my life depended on it—maybe it did.

Ironfist stood, his smirk gone. "You want to risk it? Let that tramp go to jail. Leave it alone. Is it worth your life?" He wasn't asking to be friendly or caring.

"Kill me, and they won't stop till they find Mr Chandler, whoever he is."

He laughed. "They'll never pin anything on him. They don't know who he is."

Smugness settled on my face as Bellamy stared at me, concern etched on his face. "You've been spying on Bellamy, haven't you?" Ironfist's smirk was agreement. "But you haven't been here for everything. There are some things you don't know." I was bluffing, but I wanted him to squirm, make his boss panic. "Your boss and the person who employed him are about to go down." I smiled, triumph in my eyes. Maybe I should get an acting award too.

"You're bluffing, little girl."

I raised one eyebrow. "Am I? I know you can talk to Chandler, that he can see ghosts." And there it was—the flare of surprise, then acknowledgement in his eyes. I thought about how soft and fluffy Zeus was and smiled. If the feelings behind the expressions were real, they were more believable. And I wanted him to buy it. It might force a mistake.

Ironfist swung at my face, and I leaned back. His fist just clipped my jaw, pushing my head back further, the icy sting sending a shiver all the way down my torso. Then he disappeared. Poor Bellamy; he was watching this with no idea what in Hades was going on. But I didn't have time to explain. "Charles, please come to the station. It's urgent."

He appeared. "What's up?"

"I need you to go to Rueben Solicitors in London. Go to Mr Rueben's office and spy on him. I need you to hurry back and tell me who he calls and what he says, or if he receives a call, what he says. I think Ironfist is going to warn Chandler, and he'll call Rueben. Got it?"

He nodded, excitement shining in his eyes. He smiled. "On it right now." He concentrated, probably trying to home in on the location. Thank goodness it was a business, and Charles could get access. I finally sat and looked at Bellamy as Charles popped away. "Right, Sergeant. Sorry about that, but I hope I just put things in motion."

His expression morphed from concerned to horrified. "You did what? I told you not to do anything. We can't afford to be wrong with people like that."

"This is all via ghost. They don't know what we know and what we don't. But they'll panic. Maybe they'll throw away the rest of the cyanide? Maybe they'll make phone calls to each other and the killer."

"But we don't have any DNA."

"Do another sweep of the place. Did they check the storeroom too?"

He stared at me. "Are you insinuating we didn't do a thorough job?"

"Yes, but not in a bad way." He glared, and I rolled my lips over my teeth. *Oops.* "Um, because everyone thought it was open and shut. You tested the container for cyanide, found the other container in the storeroom, but Joy was caught with the smoking gun in her hand. There were witnesses. Did you check security cameras for someone sneaking in the night before? Maybe they dropped a hair or a bit of dirt, anything. With a bit of luck, Anna hasn't mopped the storeroom since it happened."

"But what if Joy did it? I know we think she didn't because of our guts, but did we just not want to believe it of someone we interact with on a regular basis?"

I leaned forward and pinned him with my intense gaze. "But you heard everything I told you about her history with Camilla. And I did more research—her father's firm successfully defended an underworld figure in court recently. His name happens to be Ethan Robert *Chandler*."

His mouth dropped open. "You're kidding?"

I rolled my eyes. "Why would I do that? No. I'm deadly serious."

"Well, Winters, things just got a hell of a lot more complicated." He settled his elbow on the arm of his chair, rested his head in his palm, and massaged his temples.

"I also wanted to get Camilla back in to talk to Joy. Get Joy to push her on the past, get a confession. I mean, maybe the father did it off his own bat, but maybe Camilla asked him to help her. We could at least get them for conspiracy to murder with a confession, couldn't we?"

He sat up straight and ground his teeth together. "We need physical proof in court too."

"But wouldn't her confession give you a reason to get

warrants for their phone records, payment records, all sorts of things? Don't we just need enough for reasonable doubt? As far as getting Joyless out of jail anyway."

He frowned at me. "Joyless?"

"Oops, it slipped out. It's my pet name for her." I waved my hand. "Moving on. Anyway, I think if we want to get her confession, you need to call her down here now. Tell her that Joy has threatened to kill herself, and you need a friend to talk her down. I didn't expect Ironfist to be in your office. He's been spying on you, which is how I think he knows we've been looking into the case more than they wanted us to. He would've heard us mention Mr Chandler. I'm pretty sure that's where the warnings were coming from… you know, the brick. Ooh, if you could find the car that rammed me and connect it to them somehow, we'd at least get them for something."

He put his hand up. "You're going a million miles an hour. I can't keep up, Winters. Give me a moment."

I licked my bottom lip. "Just say the word, and I'll go talk to Joy. Tell her we need her to get a confession."

"How's she going to do that?"

"Goad her. Push her about what happened."

"What if it doesn't work?"

"Then it doesn't work. At least there would be nothing to blame the police for. If they wanted to target you because of what Ironfist tells Chandler, well, they'll have no real-world things to share with the press to make you look bad. There will be no paper trail."

His lips mashed together.

I stared at him, trying hard to sit still. What if we missed our chance?

He shut his eyes and scrunched up his face. Had I broken him?

After a minute, I couldn't stand it any more. "Sergeant, are you okay?

He opened his eyes. "No, I'm not okay. Damn it." Someone knocked on the door, and he yelled, "Come in!" Yep, the usually patient man had lost it.

Patel poked his head in the door. "We've got a hit on the car that struck Miss Winters. We've cobbled together different images. We found a BMW that fits the description going in a similar direction and found one that fits the timeframe. We've traced it to an industrial property in Dawlish." Did I dare hope it was the car?

"I'll arrange a warrant. Did you get a number plate?"

"There wasn't one, which was a good tip-off that it was the right black BMW."

He gave a nod to Patel, who spun around and went to do his duty. Bellamy looked at me. "Fine." He stood. "Let's go and talk to Miss Stick."

I kept my cheering to myself.

Bellamy put me in the same interview room as before and soon returned with Joy. He sat her on one side of the table, and we sat on the other. She peered at me, curiosity on her tired face. She had dark circles under her eyes, and her blonde hair had dark roots. Three of her nails had broken to the fingertip, the rest still fake and long, the polish flaking off.

"Wow, you look like crap." It was out before I realised I was saying it. "Um, sorry." Oh, God, now I was apologising to her. I wanted to roll my eyes at myself.

She laughed, and there was an edge to it. "Yeah, I look like crap. What do you expect from being in jail?" She looked from me to Bellamy. "What's this get-together about?"

"I'll let Miss Winters explain."

When Joyless's gaze hit me, I told her I'd spoken to Alan and then surmised that Camilla had done it.

Joy's eyes widened. "You really can speak to ghosts? I wasn't convinced, like I still thought it was a bit of a joke."

"Yes, I can, but if you tell anyone, I'll deny it, and Sergeant Bellamy will stick up for me." I looked at him, and he inclined his head in agreement. "Anyway,"—I didn't want to spend any time dwelling on my ability— "either Camilla asked her dad to help her, or he decided to contact someone called Mr Chandler and organised a hit without her knowledge. We need you to get a confession if possible."

She swore. "I bet it was her—she hated to lose. How could she do that to me? That makes so much sense."

I looked at her like, what the hell? "You've upset a lot of people over the years. One of them was bound to lose it. You never know when you'll choose the wrong person to pick on." My gaze was steady. I wasn't making a threat… exactly. But I wanted her to think about that in the future before she made more bad decisions. Not to save her but to save those people she targeted.

"Wow, harsh, Avery." She rolled her eyes, then stared at me. "I didn't think you were going to help me, you being one of those people you were just crying about?"

Bellamy's forehead wrinkled. It was surprising that she was being so catty in front of someone else who wasn't her BFF. "Miss Stick, Miss Winters has been kind enough to put her time into this, despite how you've treated her in the past. A bit of humility wouldn't go astray right about now. Maybe even an apology." I wished he hadn't said that last bit. An apology you had to ask for wasn't a real one.

I put up my hand. "It's fine, Sergeant. If she's not grateful, there's nothing I can do about it, but I won't be helping her again. Ever. If she can't be a decent human after all this, I'll be done wasting my time." And that was fair enough. I crossed my fingers that my need for justice and truth wouldn't overtake my good sense.

She huffed out a breath, then schooled her face to neutral. Why this was so hard for her, I had no idea. Maybe she'd had some kind of childhood trauma that made her horrible and meant that she never took responsibility for her actions. "Fine. I'm sorry, Avery. I shouldn't have treated you as I have. Thank you for helping me." There was a glint of vulnerability in her eyes that was gone even as I noticed it.

I peered at her, trying to gauge how genuine she was. I kept my guard up, but she seemed legit. "I accept your apology, Joy. Thank you."

"This doesn't make us friends, though."

I chuckled. "No, it doesn't. Don't worry."

Bellamy shook his head.

"So, now the warm and fuzzies are out of the way," I said, "we need help getting a confession out of Camilla, and we think you're just the person for the job. Will you do it?"

She sat back, an evil smile turning up her lips. "When do we start?"

CHAPTER 16

Bellamy made the call to Camilla, insisting that Joyless was suicidal and he needed her to come and talk her down. I sat across from him at his desk, biting my bottom lip and crossing my fingers that we weren't too late. If her father got wind of anything, he'd warn her, and any hope of a confession would be out the window and across the Channel.

Then there was the fact that I might be wrong about everything, but, hey, when had that ever stopped me?

Charles and Sergeant Fox popped into the office, and I jumped. Bellamy jerked his gaze to me, confusion on his face as he listened to whatever Camilla was saying. I mouthed, "Nothing."

I scowled at Charles as he sat in the chair next to me. He frowned. "What?"

I shook my head and whispered, "You scared me."

He rolled his eyes. "How was I supposed to know you'd be here? Sergeant Bellamy can't see me, so it doesn't matter if I randomly appear."

I was being unfair. "Sorry. I'm just nervous about what we're planning." I studied Bellamy's expression, waiting for the sign that she'd agreed.

"Yes. No. She's upset with her mother at the moment. You're her best friend, we understand. She'll listen to you." He nodded at something she said. As his shoulders relaxed into his chair, I smiled. "Thank you. We'll see you soon." He hung up.

I heaved out a breath. "Thank Hades for that. She sure was being difficult."

"She's in the nail salon and only half done." His sour expression told me what he thought about that. "In any case, she should be here in ten minutes. Now we just need to hope her father doesn't cotton on to what we're doing."

"When are they picking up the car?" That was the other thing that would tip them off. Once they took that car, if anyone was there, Chandler would hear about it. That, together with Ironfist's warning, would be enough to have them hurrying to close ranks.

"I'd say in another fifteen, twenty minutes." He looked at his watch, and I ignored the way his forehead wrinkled. We were cutting it fine.

I looked at Charles. "Did you find anything at Mr Reuben's office?"

"He wasn't there."

What if he was on his mobile phone right now, talking to Chandler? Sitting here doing nothing was torture. I jumped up and walked a few steps to one wall, turned, went back to my chair, and plopped down. "Argh! I can't stand the waiting." I stood again. "I'm going to the loo. Be back in two shakes."

Bellamy's face wore a pained expression. "I don't need any details, thanks, Winters."

Charles laughed, and I grinned. Sergeant Fox nodded in support of Bellamy. "Sorry, Sergeant." I almost made a joke about number ones and twos but decided he wouldn't appreciate it. Charles would, though. Missed opportunity.

After visiting the bathroom, to pass the time, I went to the break room and grabbed a coffee because it would be awesome if I was even more jittery. Would our plan work? If it didn't, I supposed we still had the car, but that wouldn't necessarily lead anyone to Mr Chandler or Camilla and her father. Knowing how crime gangs worked, whoever stored the car would take the rap for trying to run me off the road, and if they couldn't tie it to anything, they'd get little more than a dangerous driving charge. Which was tiny in the scheme of things.

So, yeah, we really needed that confession.

Coffee in hand—I probably should've asked Bellamy if he wanted one—I headed towards his office, but I halted abruptly when I spied Camilla talking to Bellamy in the office area. Coffee sloshed over the side of my cup onto the floor. *Oops.*

She had her back to me, and Bellamy studiously ignored my presence. I backed up and went into the kitchen again, poking my head out to see when he led her to the interrogation room. I took a quick gulp of my coffee, and when he opened the door and took her through, I tipped it down the sink and washed the cup.

Showtime. Yes!

We'd put a voice recording device under the table, but because we hadn't gotten legal permission or told Camilla it was being recorded, we had to be there when she made her confession, which meant Bellamy and I would wait in an adjoining room and listen in. When we thought she was going to confess, we'd quietly open the door and hear her. Bellamy was making sure she sat with her back to the door. It wasn't the best plan ever, but it was all we had.

Bellamy had explained the situation to PC Adams, who

was waiting by the security door to the cells to let me in. She checked the hallway was clear, then whispered, "Good luck."

I smiled. "We're going to need it."

My hand settled on my stomach as I made my way to the room next to our suspect. The door was ajar. I went in and sat. Bellamy shouldn't be too long. Two sets of headphones sat on the table, plugged into a small, black box that had a couple of knobs. I grabbed one of the headphones and settled it over my head. Bellamy's voice came through. "When you're finished, just press that button, and I'll come get you."

"Thank you for letting me see Camilla, Sergeant." Gratefulness dripped off Joy's words. She was a good actress.

Bellamy must've given her a nod or something because he didn't say anything, but the click of the door closing came through loud and clear. These were good headphones. I wondered what my favourite music would sound like through these. Hmm….

The man himself entered the room, shutting the door quietly behind him. He motioned for me to take the headphones off and whispered, "Are you ready?"

"As I'll ever be." I took a deep breath. "I hope this works."

"You're not the only one. Okay, let's do this."

We donned our headphones. The first part of their conversation consisted of Joyless crying. "I'm going to be in here forever. How can I live in here? I just want to die right now. Can you help me, Cammy? Please?"

"No! I'm not going to help you die. We'll find some way out of it. If you really didn't do it, surely they'll figure it out."

The crying stopped, and she huffed. "They're idiots, the lot of them. They couldn't figure their way out of a wet paper bag. They have no leads. I'm it, and only because I handed him the coffee."

"And you made it."

"Ah, thanks for the reminder." There was a pause, then Joyless's affronted voice. "You don't think I did it, do you?"

"No, no, of course not. I just… it just looks so bad. I'm sorry."

"I know I've done some terrible things in my life, Cammy, like… like what I did to you with Alan, and I'm so, so sorry. Being here has made me realise how selfish I've been to a lot of people. You were my best friend, and I betrayed you so badly. You shouldn't have forgiven me. I didn't deserve it." Oh, so she did know how to apologise when she wanted to… not that this was a real apology. This was all part of reeling Camilla in.

"It's okay. I've forgiven you. Right?" She didn't sound too sure about that.

"You're too good to me. I was just jealous. You're so gorgeous and rich and talented at polo. I-I thought if Alan could like me over you, it would prove I'm someone. You know? I didn't mean to hurt you. If I could go back in time, I would."

I swallowed. Was there a grain of truth there? Were her meanness issues down to an inferiority complex? It wouldn't surprise me. Her rawness was almost endearing, but I wasn't about to bring my walls down where she was concerned. Her future was on the line, and I was pretty sure she'd say anything if it got her out of here. But who wouldn't?

Was she going to take the bait? Would Camilla feel guilty at all? Did she even know about the framing? I shut my eyes and tried to calm myself.

"You really hurt me, Joy. I trusted you. I thought you were my friend."

"I know. You are such an awesome person. I guess this is karma for all the horrible things I've done. I know I deserve to be here, but I-I don't know if I can handle it. I really just want to die. Please, can you bring me something to do it?"

"No way! I can't. You don't want to die, Joy. Maybe they won't give you a big sentence? What if I can get my dad to defend you? His firm gets lots of people off. They're very good."

Joyless's voice wobbled. "But how can they when there's no evidence that someone else did it? I still don't understand how it happened because I swear to God that it wasn't me." Joyless sniffed. "You know that Alan broke up with me, right? He said he never got over losing you and that cheating with me was the stupidest thing he'd ever done. He never forgave me or himself, and I still love him. Now he's dead, and I'm locked up, what's left to live for?" Oh, God, if I had to listen to this soap opera much longer, I was going to go in there and get the confession out of Camilla myself.

"Did he really say he still loved me? You know, despite everything that happened, I'm so sad he's dead. I know I'm with someone else now, but I always thought Alan was the one, you know?" Bellamy and I shared a look. Why would she kill him? Was Camilla being honest right now?

My mouth went dry, the fluid draining to come out of my palms. That's how it felt, anyway. I wiped my sweaty hands on my jeans. Such a gross bodily function. It felt like my whole plan was falling apart. I hadn't anticipated this. It was reasonable to assume that Camilla would just play Joy right back, but her tone of voice was very convincing.

"I'm sorry, Cammy. I promise I didn't kill him."

"Can I ask you something?"

"Yes, of course."

"Was it… was it painful… how he died?"

I held my breath. Why was she asking? I stared at Bellamy, and he raised his brows in question. I shrugged.

Joyless sniffed. "Yes. It was horrible. He was clutching his stomach, vomiting. He even had fits on the floor. Blood came out of his nose… he was screaming. It went on for about five minutes. It was the worst thing I've ever seen." It wasn't funny, but I pressed my lips together to hold in a smile. She was exaggerating the hell out of it. I could fault Joyless for many things, but she was good at manipulation. Maybe that's why she had many people who stood by her and believed the crap that came out of her piehole when she bad-mouthed others. "And when… when he was almost dead, he cried out your name. I had to kneel next to him, but he whispered that he loved you. I-I didn't want to tell you because it broke my heart, and I didn't know how you would take it." Oh, wow, the Academy Award definitely went to Joyless for best actress in a reality drama police procedural. Again, I held my chuckle in. My propensity to laugh right now wasn't just Joyless's outstanding performance—nerves stirred in my gut that we wouldn't get the confession we needed.

"He… he did?" *Please, please, please confess.*

Bellamy's pocket buzzed. His eyes widened, and he reached into his pocket. The phone he pulled out had a sparkly pink-and-gold Gucci cover. Was that Camilla's phone? Stood to reason he'd confiscate it before she had an unsupervised chat with an inmate. Bellamy gave a slow nod at the name on the screen before turning it around so I could read it.

Dad.

I licked my bottom lip. It was a good sign that we were on the right track, and thank God Bellamy had the phone. That call could've ruined everything when we might be in the home straight.

He placed the phone on the table and looked at me, his voice muffled through my ear coverings. "I think it's time to go in." He took his earphones off and stood as Joyless's voice came through.

"He did. He loved you to the very end. If you weren't with your new man, he would've tried to get back with you. He told me that once." I stood but bent so the earphones didn't jerk off my head. This was hard to tear myself away from. Maybe I liked soap operas more than I thought.

Bellamy was at the door, and he gave me a "come on" look. I placed the headphones on the table and tiptoed out the door and into the hallway. The blind was almost all the way down on the window in the door to the next room. Bellamy had left just enough of a gap so that Joyless knew when we were outside. She was going to cry loudly to let him open the door without being heard, just in case there was any noise.

The sergeant bent and peered through the gap at the bottom of the blind. I could hear Joyless ramp up the theatrics from the hallway. Bellamy placed his hand on the handle, and my stomach clenched. He turned it slowly and painstakingly pushed the door open.

I was breathing through my mouth, trying to make no noise. If we spooked her, it would all be over.

Joyless's head was resting on her arms on the table as she cried her little black heart out. She looked up at her frenemy. "Oh, God. He was in so much pain when he died. I don't know why it happened, but there was nothing I could do to stop it. I promise I didn't do it. His poor parents. They're heartbroken. I think his mum is on suicide watch too." She sniffed loudly, and there was definitely some snot action. I cringed. Ew. "Who could do such a thing to someone? Who, Camilla?"

Camilla's shoulders shook, and she spoke through shaky breaths. "It was my fault, Joy. Can you ever forgive me?"

Joyless's eyes bugged wide. "What? Of course it wasn't. You're a good person, Camilla. The best."

She shook her head violently. "No. No I'm not. I hated you so much. So much! You stole the love of my life, and I tried to forgive you, but then you made a play for my new man, Paul. I couldn't stand it. I told my dad, and he suggested we frame you and put you in jail where you deserved to be. But he wasn't supposed to kill Alan. He was just supposed to make him sick, and they would get you on attempted murder. How did it all go wrong?" She put her head in her hands and sobbed. I was sure I heard a muffled "I'm so sorry, Alan."

I blew out a quiet, pent-up breath. Had my plan really worked? Relief seeped through my veins, warming me from head to toe.

Joyless glanced at us. Bellamy motioned for her to keep going. She put a hand on Camilla's shoulder across the table. "Wow, that's… I wasn't expecting that. But I believe you wouldn't want to kill him. I know how much you loved him."

"I did love him," she wailed. "But after what he did to me, my father hated him. He organised it through one of his clients. But Dad promised Alan wasn't going to get too sick." She raised her head and looked Joyless in the eyes. "I'm sorry, Joy. I shouldn't have gone along with it. The whole thing was wrong. You going to jail for something you didn't do. It shouldn't happen. I'm going to tell the sergeant it was me. I'm sorry."

Camilla stood and turned. Her eyes widened when she saw us. Her cheeks were wet with tears, and she wiped her arm across her nose, then held her hands out. "I helped frame Joy and kill Alan. I didn't mean for it to happen that way. Please, cuff me, Sergeant."

I stared at her. That had gone better than expected. Joyless broke her. I put my hand over my mouth. It's what I wanted, but I was still shocked. I believed her that her father was the instigator and that it went further than she wanted, but still, she'd wanted Joy out of the way. Neither of these women were very nice, and I supposed they'd been friends for a time because they understood each other.

Bellamy took a pair of handcuffs off his belt and clicked them into place on Camilla's wrists. "Camilla Reuben, you're under arrest for the murder of Alan Albertson." He looked at Joyless, who hadn't been cuffed for the meeting. "You're free to go." Bellamy grabbed Camilla's upper arm. "Please come with me, Miss Reuben."

He led her out, and I stepped out of the way. Joyless was next out of the door. She stopped and looked at me. "Thanks, Avery, and I really mean it this time." *I knew it.* Oh well…. "You didn't have to help, yet you did. I guess I owe you. I'm happy to call a truce if you are."

I hated that I felt grateful that she wasn't going to harass me any more. "Okay. I can get on board with that." I held out my hand, and she shook it.

Joy smiled. "So, I guess that's it, then. I'm out of here. Bye, Avery."

"Bye, Joy…" …*less.* I wasn't ready to fully let my guard down. I'd have to see how this panned out, and I hoped with all my heart that I hadn't just made a huge mistake in helping to free her.

Only time would tell.

CHAPTER 17

The next day, I sat in Bellamy's office, Charles and Sergeant Fox in attendance, together with the two ghosts who'd tried to infiltrate Ironfist's gang. Bellamy stared at me across the table. "So you'll tell me everything they say?"

"Yes, Sergeant. You know how it works."

"I'm learning." He gave a wry smile. "I'll start. After we arrested Camilla and she waived her right to a solicitor, her father came down and refused to let her say anything else, but once he realised what had happened, he agreed to plead guilty to everything if we gave his daughter a lighter sentence. He refused to give us any information on Chandler, though."

"Where does that leave us with him?"

Bellamy frowned. "He's a slippery sod. Been charged a few times and always wriggles free. To be honest, other than a few phone calls between the pair over the past few weeks, which doesn't prove anything since Chandler was a client of his firm, we have nothing. We also pulled security footage from the shop across the road from the night before, and it shows a dark-clad figure picking the lock of Heavenly Brew and going inside at about 1:00 a.m. We can't prove who it is, but Mr Reuben is saying it was him."

Frustration bunched my fists. "Damn. That's disappointing. What about the car that rammed me?"

"We've charged a man called Phil Braden. The car was actually stolen. Unfortunately, we can only charge him with dangerous driving with intent to injure. And he has no obvious links to Chandler or Reuben."

"Argh! They're going to get away with it." It really peed me off. I looked at the ghosts Sergeant Fox had brought. One was short and skinny, the other tall and beefy. "Did you discover anything we can use?"

They shook their heads, shame on their faces. The tall one answered. "We're sorry, Miss Winters, but we didn't have enough time to get a foothold in the group."

I sighed and relayed the message to Bellamy. I turned my attention to Sergeant Fox. "Can we keep them in there for the future? I hate that this Chandler guy is getting off scot-free."

Bellamy watched me, leaning forward, eagerly awaiting an answer. It didn't surprise me. If we could get this guy off the streets, it would come as a relief to many victims.

Sergeant Fox dropped his chin and looked at me. "Yes, Miss Winters. We were already planning on it."

I smiled at the three ghosts. "Excellent. Thank you. Your service is appreciated." The tall ghost blushed, and the short one gave a small smile.

"I take it, they're going to stay undercover?" Bellamy asked.

"You betcha. We'll get this scumbag eventually." We were stubborn. Chandler couldn't get away with things forever.

"I will warn you, Miss Winters." Sergeant Fox's gaze brooked no argument. "You're in their sights. I have no doubt that Mr Chandler and his associates were behind the attempt on your life and the warning. Don't keep provoking Ironfist if you see him. Pretend they won and you're going to back off. I would also suggest that if Sergeant Bellamy is going to speak about anything to do with Mr Chandler, that he clear it with you first. You can send Charles in to make sure Ironfist isn't in the station spying."

"That's a good idea. Thank you, Sergeant Fox." I shifted my gaze to Bellamy and repeated everything.

Bellamy looked to his side where Fox stood. "Thank you, Sergeant. Your help is greatly appreciated."

Fox looked at Bellamy. "You're doing an excellent job. I wish we could've met in person."

I told Bellamy what he said. He smiled. "Indeed. I think we would've gotten along famously."

"Oh, before I forget, have you heard back from the storage about the files on Everly's disappearance."

"Ah, yes. They're arriving next week. You're welcome to come in, and you and Patel can go through them together. He can answer any questions about evidence you're not sure about."

"Thank you so much, Sergeant." Everly wasn't going to help me, but I couldn't let it go. Despite what she thought, her mother deserved closure. "I guess that's it, then?"

"Yes, Winters. Another job well done. We'll get Chandler later. Don't worry."

"I'll try not to." I stood and looked around the room at Charles and the other ghosts, then Bellamy. "I'll see you all later. I've got work to do." I had to write up the article on the investigation, visit Zeus, and later, Carina and I were going dress shopping for the awards night.

Everyone bade me goodbye. As I walked down the corridor, the security door opened, and a woman stepped through.

Joyless's mother. I almost stopped walking and braced myself. Last time I'd seen her wasn't exactly fun. Maybe she wouldn't recognise me.

Her eyes locked on me. "Avery Winters." So much for that.

I halted. "Hello, Mrs Stick."

Her face relaxed into a smile. "I'm here to thank the sergeant, but it's good that you're here too. I wanted to apologise for my behaviour at the pub the other day. I was, as you can understand, very upset about Joy. And she mentioned you refused to help her. Anyway, I'm just grateful that you changed your mind. As I understand it, your hard work helped get my daughter out of there."

"Yes. I don't know if you know of my history with your daughter. Things haven't gone smoothly, but I didn't want to see an innocent person go to jail." Was I being rude? Who knew, but surely she would've gotten an earful from Joy when her brother got busted for vandalising my car.

"Ah, yes. I did know, which is what makes your help all the more extraordinary." She winced. "I know Joy isn't always easy to get along with. Anyway, you've gone above and beyond to help my daughter, and you should know that my whole family is in your debt. You're a wonderful person, Avery. Thank you."

I blinked back tears at her praise. My own parents had never been as kind to me as the mother of the woman who hated me. Life was weird. "It was my pleasure, Mrs Stick. I'm glad it all worked out."

And funnily enough, I really was.

Book seven in the Haunting Avery Winters series is out late 2023.

ALSO BY DIONNE LISTER

Paranormal Investigation Bureau

Witchnapped in Westerham #1

Witch Swindled in Westerham #2

Witch Undercover in Westerham #3

Witchslapped in Westerham #4

Witch Silenced in Westerham #5

Killer Witch in Westerham #6

Witch Haunted in Westerham #7

Witch Oracle in Westerham #8

Witchbotched in Westerham #9

Witch Cursed in Westerham #10

Witch Heist in Westerham #11

Witch Burglar in Westerham #12

Vampire Witch in Westerham #13

Witch War in Westerham #14

Westerham Witches and a Venetian Vendetta #15

Witch Nemesis in Westerham #16

Witch Catastrophe in Westerham #17

Witch Karma in Westerham Book #18

Witch Showdown in Westerham Book #19

Westerham Witches and an Aussie Misadventure Book #20

Book #21 (coming July 2023)

Christmissing in Westerham (Christmas novella)

Haunting Avery Winters

(Paranormal Cosy Mystery)

A Killer Welcome #1

A Regrettable Roast #2

A Fallow Grave #3

A Frozen Stiff #4

A Deadly Drive-by #5

A Caffeine Fix #6

Book #7 coming late 2023

The Circle of Talia

(YA Epic Fantasy)

Shadows of the Realm

A Time of Darkness

Realm of Blood and Fire

The Rose of Nerine

(Epic Fantasy)

Tempering the Rose

Forging the Rose

ABOUT THE AUTHOR

USA Today bestselling author, Dionne Lister is a Sydneysider with a degree in creative writing and two Siamese cats. Daydreaming has always been her passion, so writing was a natural progression from staring out the window in primary school, and being an author was a dream she held since childhood.

Unfortunately, writing was only a hobby while Dionne worked as a property valuer in Sydney, until her mid-thirties when she returned to study and completed her creative writing degree. Since then, she has indulged her passion for writing while raising two children with her husband. Her books have attracted praise from Apple iBooks and have reached #1 on Amazon and iBooks charts worldwide, frequently occupying top 100 lists in fantasy and mystery.